Zenas T. Haines

**Letters from the Forty-Fourth Regiment M.V.M.**

a record of the experience of a nine months' regiment in the Department

of North Carolina in 1862-3

Zenas T. Haines

**Letters from the Forty-Fourth Regiment M.V.M.**
*a record of the experience of a nine months' regiment in the Department of North Carolina in 1862-3*

ISBN/EAN: 9783337268077

Printed in Europe, USA, Canada, Australia, Japan

Cover: Foto ©Andreas Hilbeck / pixelio.de

More available books at **www.hansebooks.com**

FROM THE

# FORTY-FOURTH REGIMENT M. V. M. :

A RECORD OF THE

## EXPERIENCE OF A NINE MONTHS' REGIMENT

IN THE

DEPARTMENT OF NORTH CAROLINA IN 1862-3.

BY "CORPORAL."

———

BOSTON:
PRINTED AT THE HERALD JOB OFFICE, No. 4 WILLIAMS COURT,
1863.

# LETTERS.

---

In Barracks at Readville,
Saturday, Aug. 30, 1862.

Your readers in Boston will not be uninterested in following
the fortunes of the gallant 44th, which has just gone forth from
your city with full ranks, made up in large measure of young men
in whose honor and welfare every true Bostonian will feel a peculiar interest. The *personnel* of the 44th (recruited up from the Fourth Battalion of Infantry as a nucleus,) has been so frequently the subject of
newspaper remark, that nothing more need be said under that head:
but it may not be vainglorious to say that no regiment has gone forth
from the old Bay State, renowned for the quality of its soldiers, which
exceeds or equals the second New England Guard regiment, as regards the
personal qualities of its rank and file. All the learned professions are
represented in its ranks, and even some of the recondite sciences and
fine arts have their accomplished devotees in this corps. Among the
latter may be reckoned the astronomer Tuttle, of Cambridge, and the
brothers Cobb, artists, of Boston. We have sons of ministers and
millionaires, and many rich men in their own right. The sons of ministers in the 44th, grievous to say, are generally publicans themselves,
and give few signs of eminently Christian training. This is strange.

> " 'Tis true, 'tis pity;
> And pity 'tis, 'tis true."

This is the second attempt which the Fourth Battalion has recently
made to do their country some service; and we have been wondering
if the present will prove as futile as the preceding one. But these do
not cover the honorable record of the Fourth Bats. The Massachusetts 24th sprang from this Battalion. That and the 2nd and other
Massachusetts regiments of earlier and later dates have been largely officered from its ranks. It has provided the army of the Union *two*

*hundred and twenty-five commissioned officers.* A fact more extraordinary in connection with one military organization cannot be adduced, and will go far to render the Fourth historic. The youthful patriot, Putnam, whose untimely sacrifice at·Ball's Bluff, considered in connection with the unusual sweetness and force of character of the young martyr, has caused the tears of a nation to flow, was once a member of the Fourth, and his portrait now graces the walls of its armory.

The 44th came one day too soon to barrack at Readville, but it was their own fault. The fine new barracks just erected there were not completed, and will not be until to-night, although now habitable and comfortable as heart can desire. But we have all had to work to produce this comfortable state of affairs so early, and the "school of the soldier" has been neglected to-day.

Our first night in barracks was exceedingly jolly, as was to have been expected. Poor devils who depend on good sleep and a good deal of it for what vitality they can muster, might probably have sworn last night, if they had been obliged to barrack at Readville. Not that the boys were riotous, or even obstreperous, but simply jolly. We supped on hard bread, and coffee hotter than the crater of Vesuvius. Then, pipes and cigars lighted, the early evening was devoted to music — songs of home. After we had retired to our bunks, music of another character "beguiled" the hours of night.

Your correspondent slept not at all the first night in barrack, for obvious reasons. The inside musical performances opened with a barnyard chorus by the entire company, followed by a rapid, unintermitting succession of dog, hog, pig, and rooster solos, duetts and quartettes, single and combined, which continued in great volume until the unexpected arrival of the captain and his lieutenants, who are unfortunately without any ear for music. After a short intermission, the performance was resumed in a greatly modified condition, commencing with admirable imitations of chickens astray from the shelter of the maternal wing, and coming to a pause with the low, small, satisfied twitterings of chickens in clover.

Then followed sounds less artistic, but not less suggestive to the general appreciation, intermingled with snatches of conversation of a highly festive character. The good wit of the occasion rendered endurable what would otherwise have been an intolerable nuisance to any one wanting sleep so badly as your humble servant; but at last, as it must be confessed, even this element failed to satisfy a scientific audience. Objurgations, not loud but deep, came from a number of bunks where sleep had failed to come, or tarried a moment to be cruelly banished. Despite all these adverse circumstances, sound sleep actually came to one poor fellow sleeping unsuspectingly below the "Corporal:" but, as the Fates would have it, it departed from him in this wise.

A small britannia flask, used chiefly to contain coffee and milk in the temporary absence of dippers, fell from the rear of the "Corporal's" bunk directly upon the head of the sleeper, suddenly arousing him to the consciousness of life and its uncertainties. He screamed out vigorously that one of the slats of our bunk had fallen upon his head, and sarcastically offered to get up a contribution to improve our sleeping accommodations, and thereby render his own safety more complete. The "Corporal," who felt the flask slip from beneath his pillow, knew that the aroused man labored under a misapprehension, and clambered down to recover the fugitive vessel, and manipulate a suddenly prominent bump on the cranium of the one man of company D who succeeded in getting asleep.

To-day we have been applying finishing touches to our quarters, and exercising in company movements, by squads, &c. The turn-out at beat of *reveille*, this morning at five o'clock, was a new sensation even to the "Corporal." The style of the morning ablutions was a novelty, too. Instead of basins and soap at the barracks, we were ordered to "fall in with towels," and then were positively marched to a pond to wash our faces and hands! O, the degradation of military rule! Such is war.

To-morrow we shall look for a host of friends from Boston. We will not attempt to disguise the hope we cherish, that they may bring their pockets full of apples!

In the multiplicity of Colonels Lee, never *lees* in a military sense, your correspondent may inform somebody by stating that the Colonel Lee commanding the 44th, was Major Lee of the 4th Battalion, and never Colonel Lee of the 20th or 27th, or Colonel Lee of the Governor's Staff, but is a brother of the latter. He is a large-hearted man, and a splendid officer. His staff and line officers are fully worthy of him. Altogether we are eminently satisfied with ourselves as a regiment.

---

IN BARRACKS AT READVILLE, }
SEPT. 6, 1862. }

Our first Sunday in barracks was enlivened by the presence of friends from Boston. The hope we breathed with respect to apples was more than met. The last cigar in many a private stock had just ended in smoke, and shed its sweetness on the desert air of Readville, haply to be succeeded by new relays at the hands of thoughtful friends. Wine, fruit and other comestibles poured into some favored messes with overwhelming abundance, and it must be confessed that Monday's bill of health was not improved by Sunday's too luxurious bill of fare. "Corporal" would suggest that pastry and cake are of no benefit to a soldier, but that ripe fruit is not only a luxury, but of great advantage as a corrective of the system.

Another sanitary suggestion. Several sick men on Monday traced their ill health to bathing too soon after dinner. Few men can safely plunge into the water within four hours after eating heartily. It stops the digestive machinery, and then all goes wrong, indefinitely. Just before dinner is a good time to bathe, or just before breakfast or supper will do.

Would any one like to know how our first dress parade went off? Well, I shan't tell. The occasion was graced by the Boston Brass Band; but a spirited young horse in front of the lines did the best thing of the day — dancing in perfect time to the music. With his head erect and nervously distended nostrils, he was a picture of grace. That that horse has a soul "Corporal" has no doubt, else how could he have music in it? Horses of duller metal were all around him, standing upon three legs, and doing nothing but switch their tails at the flies. Some human beings behave still more indifferently at concerts.

There is some emulation among the companies in the way of neatness, conveniences and decorations about their several barracks. The palm is due to Company D for an early display of flags upon the outside, and also for certain novel decorations of the interior in the shape of one or two delicate articles of apparel, probably wafted by the wind from a washing hung out to dry.

One of our fellows was attacked by a cow the other day, and badly wounded in his under-garments, but is expected to recover.

Company D has paid a little compliment to its commissioned officers. Captain Sullivan was made the recipient of a sword, sash, and belt, and to Lieutenants Blake and Stebbins were presented shoulder straps. These gentlemen are justly beloved by the men of their company for their entire devotion to duty, and their high accomplishments as officers. They are all graduates of the Fourth Battalion. Of the qualifications of Captains Hunt, Lombard and Kendall also, the personal acquaintance of your correspondent enables him to speak in terms of high praise.

Company F having had the temerity to erect a flag-staff taller than Company D's, the latter company extended its mast a few feet over that of its neighboring barrack. This ambition to excel exhibits itself in a variety of ways. Some of the barracks are prettily lighted with lanterns, and in one or two of them the bunks are lettered and ornamented in a very artistic manner. Afterward Captain Spencer Richardson's boys secured the tallest pole which could be found in the neighboring woods, and at the present writing their flag floats the highest. The barracks occupied by the companies of Captain Lombard, Captain Hunt and Captain Kendall also have creditable displays of bunting, and contribute to give the encampment an animated and beautiful appearance.

Each company has its excellent choir of singers, but Company F affords instrumental as well as vocal music. The Cobb brothers, who are excellent violinists, nightly delight a numerous auditory assembled about their bunks.

As our stay at Readville protracts, we are gathering about us many little comforts and luxuries which we shall probably have to sacrifice in the event of a sudden retirement from before an enemy. But while we stay here our purpose is to make ourselves extremely comfortable; and in this purpose a numerous constituency of friends are lending their assistance in the way of hampers and baskets and bundles of fruit, and other delicacies. Our mess gratefully acknowledges a basket of incomparable pies from a pious lady in Boston, who has no peer among modern pastry cooks. Our judgment condemns all such luxuries, but our heart acknowledges how good they are. And we are most generously remembered in gifts of more substantial value—writing desks, medicines, wax-tapers, smoking caps, pipes, tobacco, cigars, &c., &c. All these, we know, are the romance of war, the pleasant prelude of things considerably rougher, but we will enjoy them while we may, and when we come to the sterner duties of the soldier our hearts and arms shall be nerved to strength by all the thoughtful kindness which friends now lavish upon us.

We shall not forget the " Donation Committee" of the city of Boston, or its queenly agent who presides at the headquarters on Tremont street, and dispenses havelocks, Testaments, pins, needles, towels, handkerchiefs, &c., to every applicant whom it is in her power to serve.

I informed you in my first letter that our regiment was honored by the membership of the astronomer Tuttle; I omitted, however, to mention that he rejected the tender of a lucrative position in the Washington Observatory to do a private soldier's duty in the 44th Regiment.

Patriotism more self-sacrificing than this is rarely to be found, but when found, a note should be made of it at once. We propose to call our astronomical comrade "Old Stars." Although not yet twenty-three years old, he has already grown gray in his assiduous night-watches for the starry voyagers of the upper deep; and now his chief anxiety is to be placed upon the round of the night sentinel, where he may pursue his favorite study.

We have been having some delicious days this week. It was pleasure enough to live in such atmosphere and sunlight. Our evenings, too, have been delightful, and we have had with them the music of the band, promenades, dancing, &c. Many friends, with beautiful turnouts, and without, have visited us, and we have had a wonderfully happy week. Who shall describe the wonderful beauty of these September sunrises, and the exhilaration of the morning air and bath at the pond?

On Thursday we were honored by a visit from a sub-committee of the Citizens' Committee of Boston, deputed to investigate the cuisine of this regiment. Reports had gone abroad that we were badly fed; that, in point of fact, we were not allowed broiled chickens for breakfast, nor roast beef and plum-pudding for dinner. It is barely possible that the committee had even more serious charges to investigate, and were horrified to discover that we had neither loaf-sugar or cream in our tea and coffee. Notwithstanding these serious deficiencies, the committee were constrained to confess that our bread and soup were good enough for the guests of the Parker House, and that in all other respects we fared as well as the soldiers of any other regiment. We certainly didn't know that we were badly used, until we were honored by the visit of the gentlemen of eminent gravity. We *would* whisper one word in the ear of the cook, and ask him to cook the rice; but for the consolation of that amiable individual we would remind him of the remark of Thomas Jefferson, that there was but one woman north of the Potomac who knew how to perform this important culinary operation.

The time of our departure, as well as our destination, is still problematical. Some have it that we are going to Virginia, others to Baltimore, others to New Orleans, and others that we are to remain where we are for a considerable space of time. The work of drill has commenced in earnest, and in a few weeks, few regiments will excel the 44th in thoroughness of instruction. We have received our guns (Enfield rifles), although they have not yet been distributed. A portion of our uniforms have arrived, and will soon be distributed. A large number of the regiment will wear uniforms made to measure, and of better stock than that furnished by Uncle Sam.

Before we leave Readville, it is suggested that we give our friends a grand parting reception and ball, and that an acre or two of the camp-ground be floored over for the convenience of those who would like to trip the light fantastic.

————

IN BARRACKS AT READVILLE,
SEPT. 13, 1862.

It may interest your readers to know that the field occupied by the 44th Regiment is where the famous striped pig was exhibited twenty odd years ago—the pig made immortal in the well-remembered song commencing—

> "In Dedham just now there was a great muster,
> Which gathered the people all up in a cluster;
> A terrible time, and what do you think,
> To find a way to get something to drink!
> Ri tu, di nu, di nu," &c.

To-day traffickers in the ardent hereabout labor under similar embarrassments with those of 1840. Colonel Lee has military jurisdiction over a territorial radius of one mile, and has no bowels of compassion for those fellows who open rum and refreshment booths along the highways and in the bushes about the camp. "Corporal" has already signalized himself by leading a squad of men and assisting in the confiscation and reduction of a liquor shanty romantically situated among the pines in the vicinity. The operation yielded us one flask of whisky, two empty flasks, and a fresh supply of needed lumber, whereof "Corporal" was awarded one board in consideration of his gallantry on the occasion alluded to.

Another new sensation has befallen your correspondent in his first experience as corporal of the guard. We have had a succession of magnificent days and nights since we went into camp, and guard duty has not been the most disagreeable part of our experience as soldiers. The calm majesty of these moon-lit nights, the brooding stillness occasionally broken by the challenge of the sentinel in this and the neighboring camps, and the white tents and garrisons dotting the dark field, conspire to form a scene of impressive beauty.

We have received an order from the Commander-in-Chief of all the forces in Massachusetts prohibiting us from bathing at all Christian hours of the day, out of regard to the sensitive nerves of somebody. As nobody but soldiers live near the ponds, it is to be supposed that the order was promulgated as a measure of consideration of the naiads and nymphs habitant hereabout. We heartily wish that everybody was like Cæsar's wife.

The " women of America," including a few Boston friends, have sent us in a grand lunch of Washington pies, coffee and cold meats. Where these dainties went to is a profound mystery to the non coms. and privates, but it is doubtless " all right."

At dress parade, the other day, Miss Josie Gregg, of Boston, through Colonel Lee, presented us an elegant flag, and the gift was acknowledged by three cheers. Captain Spencer Richardson has received a sword, sash, &c., from friends of the Mercantile Library Association, of which he is an ex-president. Orderly Stebbins, of Company F, brother of Lieutenant Stebbins, of Company D, has received a sword, sash, &c., from members of his company. Dan. Simpson, the drummer, has received from friends in Company C (Captain Lombard), a Turkish fez, which gives old Dan. a very rakish appearance.

Flag competition continues, and now every barrack shows its bunting — that of Company D again floating the highest. Thursday morning Company F's flag-staff presented to the eyes of an astonished camp the same small white, bifurcated garment which had previously served to decorate the interior of a neighboring barrack. The boys are bound not to " 'have their selves," as Uncle Sim Wilbur used to say. We now hope, however, for better things for our company, having sent the sergeants to a tent by themselves, and conferred the responsibility of keeping good order upon the corporals.

Captain James Richardson's company give their barrack a beautiful, almost oriental appearance at evening, by the introduction of numerous Chinese lanterns. In every barrack the fine arts are still cultivated in the lettering and ornamentation of the bunks. One is labelled " Squirrels' Nest ;" another, " Penguin's Nest ;" another, " Sleeping Beauties ;" another, " Siamese Twins ;" another, " Damon and Pythias." Some graduates of Tufts College, who occupy a bunk together, inform the world in good classical phrase that it is sweet to die for your country. They may well say that, if living in the barracks at Readville be dying for your country. " Corporal " cannot but look with amazement upon these classical young patriots elevated upon their bunks and devouring home danties over this conspicuous motto — " *Dulce et decorum est pro patriæ mori !*"

In Company D we have the following graduates and under-graduates of Tufts College : — E. Fitz Gerald, Portsmouth, New Hampshire ; C.

Adams, Middleton, North Carolina: J. B. Brewster, Plymouth; W. E. Savery, South Carver: W. C. Ireland, Boston; W. E. Gibbs, West Cambridge, Massachusetts; W. P. Treat, Canton, Maine; and A. C. Fish, Janesville, Wisconsin. As may be supposed they are ornaments to the company and regiment. Mr. Gibbs relinquishes the pastorate of the Universalist Church in West Cambridge and a liberal salary to serve his country as a private soldier.

Our Chaplain, Rev. Mr. Hall, of Plymouth, was introduced to us last Sunday, and made a good impression upon the regiment for his brevity of speech and avoidance of religious cant. He said the engrossing duty of the day was devotion to our country, and felicitated the young men of the regiment that an opportunity was opened to them to consecrate their powers to so high an object. The music was very hum-drum, considering the number and quality of our vocalists, but we shall do better.

Mr. Charles White, of Milton, who has two sons in the 44th, is getting up a regimental song book. Original contributions of the true ring would doubtless be well received.

The quarters of Company G, Captain Hunt, are tastefully ornamented with evergreen, and are much admired by visitors; but it is on all hands conceded that the barrack of Company D, thanks to the oversight of our admirable Corporal Waterman, is most noticeable for its complete order and neatness. It is whispered that we are to have a piano, if we remain here much longer; and then, with such singers among us as Charley Ewer, from the Warren Street choir, we reckon upon very good times in the musical line.

Yesterday was a great day with the men of the 44th. We were mustered into the service of the United States by companies. The event was hailed with cheering and general rejoicing; and then the uniforms provided by Uncle Sam were opened for inspection. Many members of the regiment had already provided themselves with garments of superior quality, made to measure, and those who had not taken this precaution regretted it the more when they came to see the half cotton, shoddy, slouchy stuff sent to them through the State authorities. Colonel Lee, who has a natural abhorrence of shams in all shapes, advised his men not to draw such uniforms, and promised to assist them in procuring garments made to measure. The men gladly acted upon the suggestion of the Colonel and will clothe themselves, not less as a matter of neatness and taste than of economy.

The mustering-in certificates were given out yesterday and to-day, and some of the boys have already pocketed the generous bounties voted them in Boston and elsewhere. Mayor Wightman was here on Friday, and was cheered as he passed among the barracks.

Last evening the barrack of Company F, Captain Storrow, was the centre of attraction. The parents of the artists Cobb were present, and the delighted spectators of a country break-down and other festive demonstrations. Mrs. Cobb delivered a little impromptu poem, and Mr. Cobb a very stirring address, both of which were vociferously applauded. The Cobb brothers sang and played exquisitely, and the occasion was one of touching interest.

Brigadier-General Pierce has been appointed to command Camp Meigs, including the several encampments at Readville, and Lieutenant Richard H. Weld, Post Adjutant.

To-day a fine flag-staff was erected at the brigade headquarters near the depot. In a little while Camp Meigs will be one of the grandest and most complete military posts in New England.

We have been provided with muskets for guard duty only, and of course have much work to perform in the manual of arms' drill before we shall be fit to take the field. In the facings we have made commendable progress, and have been highly complimented by Colonel Lee in this respect.

Since the 44th went into barracks they have been favored with the services of the Boston Brass Band, under the lead of Mr. Flagg. It is said the expense is to be defrayed by an assessment upon the regiment. Considering that the mass of the regiment have had no voice in the selection of a band, a number of persons are inclined to consider this a little " rough."  What " Corporal" and many others wish to suggest in this connection is, that a few of our rich friends in Boston unite to defray the expense of a *good* band, which shall accompany us to the seat of war. It is thought they would be pleased to confer this substantial benefit upon the regiment, and thus acknowledge the important assistance rendered by the Fourth Battalion of Infantry in raising the quota of Boston. Failing in this, a set of instruments would be gratefully acknowledged, and an excellent band would then be recruited from the regiment.

----

IN BARRACKS AT READVILLE,  }
SATURDAY, Sept. 20, 1862.  }

We begin to feel the rigors of a soldier's life, and among our hardships are green corn, onion soup, baked beans, brown bread, boiled potatoes, &c. If we had not been mustered in at the time we were, there is no saying what the consequences of delay might not have been. As for our cook, he has been forced to seek an asylum out of camp, under a pretence of sickness. He could no longer face the frown of a virtuous and half-starved soldiery, so he unwreathed his face of "that smile," which had so long deceived the boys, and then—

"Folded up his dishcloth like the Arabs,
And in darkness stole away."

Applications for the vacancy at the "Bite Tavern," from Parker & Mills and J. B. Smith are under consideration.

Since we were sworn in we have felt the tightening of the military rein. No man has been allowed to see his friends, or to receive presents from them except on the points of their bayonets. On Monday about two hundred men only could be mustered for battalion drill. The other eight hundred, except those who had gone to Boston and elsewhere, were in irons at the guard-house. Colonel Lee and staff were intoxicated — with the varied strains of the Boston Brass Band. Altogether we have been in a sad muss.

When are we going to leave for the seat of war? We don't know. It is said at the Adjutant-General's office that we shall be the next regiment to leave. If this is so, why are not the muskets given out? The Elementary Spelling Book used to say, "wheels are admirable instruments of conveyance." It might also have said that guns are useful implements of warfare, and that wheelings and facings alone never did kill the devil. "Corporal," who confesses to a distaste for actual warfare, and who, like Sparrowgrass, would be glad never to leave his State, except in case of invasion, indulges the hope that this delay in distributing the arms indicates an indefinite continuance of barrack life and drill.

The past week has been one of furloughs, the men being thus enabled to go to their several hailing places and procure their bounties. We are sorry to say that red tape has ruled potently with some of the town authorities, and that some soldiers have been disappointed in not receiving what is clearly theirs, for the want of forms of certificate not required in Boston. Dear old Boston! She not only does generous things, but does them as quietly and with as little trouble to the recipients as though she was not conferring a benefit. She that never tires in doing good is not mis-named "the Hub." "Corporal" will be her spokesman, although his bounty came not from her treasury, nor any other, as yet.

We reasonably expect that a week of furloughs will be succeeded by work. Some of our little captains are threatening us hard. More drill and less guard duty will not be unacceptable to the poor fellows, whose duty as sentinels for the past week has only been relieved by the relaxation of police guard work or scavenger service. Bootless has been the plea, " I was on guard yesterday, and police guard the day before." The orderly knew it. There was no help for it. It costs hard work, but we have the cleanest camp in Christendom, if we may believe visitors. Lieutenant McLaughlin, our mustering-in officer, was profuse in his commendations of the 44th. It was, he said, the most orderly and the cleanest regiment he ever mustered in. The company rolls were the neatest which had ever come under his inspection, and the number of absentees (one sick and one unavoidably absent,) the smallest in his experience. We do not wish to be always elevating our horn, but we must record history.

Speaking of guard duty, we have added to our guards another wheel in the camp machinery of good order—a provost guard. Captain Smith, of Company H, has been appointed Provost Marshal of this post. Lieutenant Forbes, of Company K, formerly of the Commercial Bulletin, Lieutenant Laughton, of the 43d Regiment, and Lieutenant Singleton, of the 42d, have been appointed Lieutenants of the provost guard. The headquarters of this guard are near the depot. It consists of a relief from each of the above regiments, and its principal duty is to reduce rum booths in the vicinity and look up stragglers from the camp.

Since my last letter there have been added to the list of decorated barracks those of Company B, Captain Griswold, and Company A, Captain Richardson. Company D has introduced Chinese lanterns, small flags, and the arms of the New England Guards, neatly painted by one of our numerous artists, to wit, Fred. Sayer, the lingual prodigy and pet of his corps. We have not yet procured a drummer, but our tallest corporal, Messinger, who has seen enough of military preferment, is in training as a candidate. Since the above was written, a drummer has been selected, but Messinger's claims were ignored.

Among the testimonials of the past week have been a sword, sash and belt to Orderly Hatch, of Captain Hunt's company, and a splendid meerschaum pipe to Captain James Richardson. Gold, silver and amber combine to make the latter present a dudheen of irreproachable beauty.

A startling rumor has just come into camp to the effect that we are to be allowed no more extras. The fellows who have been subsisting upon pies, sponge cake, pickles, etc., etc., propose to hold an indignation meeting, and arouse public sentiment against the contemplated outrage. If we cannot be allowed to eat *Washington* pies, what are our liberties worth, we should like to know? More than this, we are not to be allowed to eat our rations in barrack except in rainy weather. Such is war. But are we to be kept under stricter discipline than regiments in the field? Are we to have no sutler? Is the dealer in "vegetable oysters" opposite the guard house to be driven off? We refuse to believe it.

A large proportion of the regiment is now uniformed in neatly fitting suits, having no relationship to the contractors' shoddy which was attempted to be foisted upon us. Our appearance at the dress parades is creditable, and every pleasant afternoon crowds of spectators honor us with their presence. The number of pretty girls that adorn these occasions, coming as they do, laden with offerings of fruits and flowers for their favorites, is by no means the least interesting feature of the afternoon displays. The angels even besiege us in our barracks, and although we are delighted to see them, they seem sometimes to forget that we have no retiring rooms, and that we must perforce make our toilettes in our bunks, or not make them at all. "Corporal" wants it distinctly understood that he don't care anything about this, personally. He speaks for the modest man of his company.

Yesterday the numerous flags at Camp Meigs were at half-mast in respect to the memory of General Reno. To-day the Warren Drum Corps were rapturously received by the soldiers of the 44th. Doctor Kirk, the great and earnest-hearted minister of the Mount Vernon Church, was in camp to-day, distributing neat little books appropriate to soldiers. Neatly printed *books* are read when mere tracts are thrown away. "Corporal" heard one fellow remark with irreverent facetiousness that somebody had filled his booth with tracts and carried away all articles of extrinsic value. The chap had undoubtedly lost something, and selected this profane way of giving vent to his anger.

Your correspondent could expatiate by the half column of the social fascinations of this life in barracks, of the genial friendships formed; of the glorious hearts discovered; of the roaring wit brought out by this free and easy companionship; of the freedom from conventional restraints and the care of every-day pursuits. Do not, dear reader, think us too jolly and comfortable for soldiers, but rather thank Heaven for the sunny side and recompense of military life, which, perhaps, after

all, but very feebly offset the shadows through which lies the pathway
of him who takes up arms in defense of liberty, imperilled as it is
to-day.

———

IN BARRACKS AT READVILLE,
SATURDAY, SEPT. 27, 1862.

One of our home corps was at Camp Meigs last Sunday, and noted
the extraordinary rush of visitors upon that day.  The members of the
44th were allowed a few hours' leave of absence outside their lines, and
improved the time by visiting the encampments of the other regiments
and battery east of the pond.  The visit was an agreeable one, and afforded us a fine opportunity to contrast the condition of our camp with
that of the other regiments at this post.  We found the barracks of the
45th (Cadet Regiment) in fine condition, and constructed with better
regard to light and ventilation than our own.  In other respects we did
not suffer by comparison with either regiment.  Gilmore's Band honored us by playing the Fourth Battalion Quickstep.  Gilmore promises
us a serenade one of these fine evenings.  In a few days more we shall
have more moonlight nights, and, if we remain at Camp Meigs, a repetition of out-door evening sociability, music and moonlight rambles.  At
this writing, however, the air is thick with rumors of a speedy departure
of our regiment.  We have it from apparently good authority that the
47th, Colonel Marsh, is to occupy these barracks next week, and that a
transport now lies in Boston harbor waiting to convey us to New Orleans, or Newbern, for one of which posts, it is said, we are to sail the
latter part of next week.  Another rumor sends us to Annapolis, preliminary to our sea voyage South, and another to Fort Warren.  We
propose to resign ourselves to either of these dispositions, especially to
the New Orleans trip, now that we begin to feel the bite of these au-
tumn nights and mornings.  The most unmusical of sounds is the *reveille*
at five o'clock, A. M.  Even the freshness and magnificence of those
star-gemmed mornings scarcely compensate us for this ghostly hour of
turning out.  But now we are threatened with calls among the small
hours for the purpose of preparing us for surprises in the enemy's
country.  We would gladly excuse our officers from this laborious work
in our behalf.  In fact, we shall not be less grateful to them if they do
not carry the plan into execution.  Beside, midnight movements like
these might excite the suspicion of our ubiquitous provost guard,
and result in getting the whole regiment into limbo.  We could not

even visit our neighbors of the other regiments, last Sunday, without falling into the hands of those merciless Philistines, who go about the country like roaring lions seeking whom they may devour.

Companies E and D have been making double-quick marches to Dedham village by the three-mile route. An uninterrupted run of three miles is something incredible to the uninitiated. "Corporal" and five others confess, with proper self-abasement, that the last mile was rather too much for them, especially as your correspondent was tortured by a pair of new boots. We fell out. The first man who "caved in" was *Tucker*—a coincidence worthy the notice of one of your cotemporaries. By seasonably falling out, we escaped rushes of blood, palpitations of the heart, and further abrasions of the feet, but we were soon placed in mortal terror of the provost guard. We saw their blue habiliments and burnished muskets in the distance, and rushed precipitately into the first wayside building. They did not discover us, but we saw their wagon enter the village of Dedham close upon the heels of those who had out-winded us. We fondly hoped that our comrades would get arrested — so amiable is human nature; but the guard saw their formidable numbers and passed by on the other side. In the place where Tucker and his fellow recusants sought seclusion, we were hospitably regaled with apples, and then soon after started upon our return to camp by another road. A tint of blue in the distance re-awakened our fears of the provost. We rushed into a barn and peeped through half-closed doors, until a lady in cerulean garb drove past and relieved us of our immediate terror. A little further along, the familiar notification of "vegetable oysters and refreshments" induced us to invest in a bottle of pop beer. "Vegetable oysters," although loudly demanded, were not to be had. At last the ill-disguised scorn of the woman who kept the place recommended us to leave. Who should we next encounter but two soldiers? They doubtless belonged to the provost: but we put a bold face upon the matter, and determined to stand the chances. They were *not* the provost. They might think we were, so we demanded their passes in the most business-like manner we could assume, and they were produced, although not without manifest distrust of our functions. We pronounced the passes satisfactory, and then proceeded camp-ward with aching sides and manifestations of severe colic, which further excited the suspicions of the two artillerymen with passes. A little while before dinner, a small "awkward squad" might have been seen descending the railroad embankment near Camp Meigs, and then proceeding, crab-like, by the right and left flanks, until it safely passed the lines. The main party had not arrived, and we confidently reported them in the hands of the provost. On the contrary, as we learned upon their arrival, they had been detained by a number of beautiful Samaritans habitant along the road, who came out laden with apples and pears, which were distributed among the soldiers with smiles and kind words. Several fellows came back to camp with hearts and pedal extremities equally damaged.

Our rifles have been distributed at last, and we have commenced drilling in the manual with great industry. We are going strictly by "the book," and have to unlearn some things peculiar to the tactics of Colonel Stevenson, formerly of the Fourth Battalion. This gentleman, by the way, visited us on Wednesday, and was cordially received. If he had arrived at the time he was expected, a formal demonstration by the entire regiment would have been made in his honor. We were all drawn up in line for that purpose, but it is not improbable that "Tom," as his old military *confreres* fondly call him, got wind of the proceeding.

The rumors given in my last concerning stricter camp discipline were chiefly true. We are not allowed to eat in the barracks. The order concerning extras from home has not been rigidly enforced, and our friends have been allowed to remember us with many little comforts, and to assist at many delightful messes in the company streets. As a screw has lately worked loose in the matter of rations, it must be confessed that these attentions from our friends have proved most fortunate. Some of the boys will have it that the interests of the regimental sutler were consulted in the late promulgation about provisions in the barracks, and several companies have voted not to patronize that individual. It is certainly difficult to conceive why dainties from home are more objectionable in a military point of view than those from the sutler's stores. In this connection, "Corporal" would state that Company D, in the matter of rations, owes much to the liberality of Corporal Page.

On Thursday we had a grand cleaning out of barracks. Everything was removed from them, and exposed to the air and sunshine. Most of the regiment being absent on escort duty, the task devolved upon a few. It was a work of vandalism. Cherished shelves, pictures, flags, and flowers came down at one fell swoop. The personal effects of absentees were tumbled down and bestowed in promiscuous piles into the bunks, and then carried outside. They comprised a heterogeneous collection of valuables, like pats of butter, soap, packs of cards and Testaments, tooth-brushes and cutlery, spare clothing and baskets, haversacks, havelocks, night-caps and smoking-caps, pipes, tobacco and matches, now and then a bottle, and one umbrella. Having the example before them of the army in Flanders, the absentees of the 44th swore when they came back and witnessed the "improvements" which had been made while they were away.

We have occasional evening entertainments here in the shape of ground and lofty tumbling (*in costume*) and sparring matches. Between our hours of drill, camp duties, reception of visitors, music, letter-writing, &c., there is no possibility of time dragging upon our hands. Now visitors are restricted to the hours between half past four and half past eight P. M. Among the testimonials of the past week was the presentation to Orderly Tripp, of Company D, (Captain Sullivan) of a beautiful sword, sash and belt. The company are much attached to their orderly for his modest and efficient way of performing the many and arduous duties appertaining to his post. Orderly Sumner, of Captain Kendall's company, who is also highly spoken of, has received a similar compliment.

Our Surgeon, Dr. Ware, of Boston, is drawing a tight rein over the regiment. His experience upon the Peninsula has given him notions of sanitary discipline which some think too severe for soldiers in barracks at home. He has stripped our quarters of everything but prime necessaries, and we are reduced to a very bald condition indeed. We shall probably see the wisdom of this severity more clearly by and by. At present a majority of the boys don't see it at all. Thursday night we tried the experiment of sleeping without straw in our bunks. It didn't work, and now we propose to provide ourselves with canvas bags to keep the straw in place, and thus avoid the continual nuisance of straw litter inside and out.

On Thursday detachments from six companies of our regiment acted as escort at the funeral of the late Lieutenant-Colonel Dwight. Considering the short time of our practice in the manual of arms, the regiment was awarded the credit of great proficiency, particularly in the firing of vollies. Colonel Stevenson paid the regiment the highest compliment.

Among other things for the convenience of the soldiers is the arrangement made by Brigadier-General Pierce to have two regular mails daily. Letters directed "Camp Meigs, Boston," with the letter of the company and the number of the regiment, will reach their destination promptly. Mails close in Boston at seven A. M., and two P. M. The arrangement thus far has worked admirably.

The Brigadier was serenaded last night by our band, which went to his quarters, accompanied by the Colonel, staff and line officers, all of whom received the hospitable courtesies of the commanding General.

On Friday the old members of the Fourth Battalion were pleased to witness the beaming countenance of ex-Adjutant Soule, late military superintendent of plantations in South Carolina. Mr. Soule was Adjutant of the Battalion when it was sworn into the United States service last May. He now declares his intention of going with us as a private soldier. We shall be glad to welcome him into our ranks.

In closing this letter, "Corporal" must acknowledge a kind and most substantial remembrancer from a noble woman in Clinton, whose gift was accompanied by a note full of sentiments of patriotism, and personal interest in the soldier. Her kindness will not be forgotten by your correspondent or his " mess."

----

In BARRACKS AT READVILLE, }
SATURDAY, OCT. 4, 1862. }

The past week Col. Lee has wisely varied our drill by taking the regiment on marches through portions of the country surrounding Camp Meigs. Our first of these marches, after escort duty at the funeral of the late Lt. Col. Dwight, was through that portion of Milton of which we have such delightful glimpses from the camp. We were forced to breathe dust freely, but through the clouds which rose wherever the regiment moved we caught refreshing views of stately homesteads, blushing orchards, and autumn-tinted landscapes. We were halted a mile from camp, and treated to cool water in front of an elm-shaded farm house overlooking a bend in a smooth stream just where a herd of cows were enjoying their forenoon delectation. If they had arranged themselves for picturesque effect they couldn't have done better. If the reader would see apples upon the wayside trees "like apples of gold in pictures of silver," let him take a warm, dusty march of six miles past orchards laden with September fruitage. Since the march to Milton we have surprised the good people of Mill Village and round about Dedham Court House by a sudden appearance in their midst. For the gratification of our many friends who are anxiously watching the progress of this regiment, I have to report that our marching extorted great praise from Col. Lee, who, by the way, is quite as prompt to give us a sound blowing up as he is to compliment. In point of fact, he does neither by halves. His outspoken frankness and generosity are creating him hosts of warm friends in the regiment.

Our camp has not been without one or two episodes of "romance in real life," to coin a phrase.  Last Sunday—a day exactly answering to the description of the poet—

"——sad, and dark, and dreary,"—

the camp of the 44th was visited by a pale fair one in quest of her "betrayer." Betrayer, a moustached young fellow not unknown among the Boston sports, attempted to play the stranger.  The dodge was unsuccessful.  The young woman proclaimed that he was her lovyer, and moustache was finally obliged to succumb.  They met at the guard house.  What passed between them is not known, but enough was guessed at to seriously affect the sensibilities of the susceptible young sergeant on duty upon that occasion.  After the interview, the young woman started to leave the field, but being overtaken by a real fainting fit, was brought back by a corporal's guard, and a new opportunity was thus afforded the gallant lieutenants at that post to render any assistance which the circumstances might require.  Lieut. Forbes especially signalized himself by his delicate attentions; and it should be mentioned that a large number of other lieutenants signified their willingness to be serviceable in the same direction.  "Corporal" is happy to be assured that the young woman is likely to survive her rather doubtful heart-wounds.

Since the above was written, it is rumored that the parties are man and wife.

There is no great harmony in camp upon the subject of music.  A proposition to defray the future expense of the Boston Brass Band at the rate of five cents a day per man was not agreed to.  Many of us will be sorry to lose the band, which acquits itself very creditably, but we shall have left to us the consolation of Dan Simpson's drum and the veteran Smith's fife.  For sixty odd years has the latter been without a peer upon the instrument he uses, and now it does the soul good to hear his trills at *tattoo* and *reveille*, as we stand in the company street for roll-call.  May he never be without something to wet his whistle !

We received marching orders last Thursday, and are going to Newbern, N. C., as soon as a transport vessel can be got in readiness.  At Newbern it is expected we shall be brigaded under General, now Colonel, Stevenson.  This will be gratifying to the regiment.

"Corporal" is requested to correct a statement which crept into his last letter to the effect that private Tucker, of Co. D, was the first to cave in on the late double-quick march to Dedham. It should have read "one of the first." Your correspondent has no desire to sacrifice truth to a pun. Tucker is doubtless a man of bottom as well as speed.

Among the testimonials to officers in the 44th should be mentioned the presentation of a sword, sash and belt to Orderly Cunningham, of Company C, and a sword, sash, belt and pistol to Orderly Buck of Company B.

Our indefatigable surgeon is organizing and training a corps of assistants who are to lend their aid to the wounded upon the field of battle. The training consists of binding up imaginary wounds, pointing out the position of arteries, showing how to handle fractured limbs, placing men upon litters, and showing how to carry them with the least possible disturbance of the wounded parts.

Since my last the ventilation of the barracks has been improved by sawing out holes in the walls, close to the floors. This is going to the bottom of the matter. The idea of getting rid of carbonic acid gas by forcing it up through the sky-lights is an exploded one, and ought to be forced out of the minds of those who argue that "bad air rises."

Mr. Steffen, formerly a captain in the Prussian service, and recently instructor of the Massachusetts Rifle Club, is a frequent visitor to our regiment, and is now delivering a series of military lessons to our officers. Mr. Steffen is a well educated gentleman, and a military instructor of decided accomplishments.

Since Lieutenant Forbes signalized himself by his gallantry to a distressed fair one, he has figured less agreeably in another affair, and has resigned his commission. His offense appears to have been in putting too much stress upon the subordination due from privates to non-commissioned officers, especially corporals. His language, it must be confessed, was more forcible than elegant, and bordered too strongly upon the profane to escape the censure of Colonel Lee, who asked the lieutenant to resign or submit to a court-martial.

Yesterday and to-day short furloughs have been freely granted, and there is a general impression that they are our last ones. We may not, however, leave for a week or two yet.

Your correspondent notices in the Boston Advertiser the following statement concerning Company F, Captain Storrow, of the 44th Regiment, which was prepared by a member of that company. The men were measured in their stockings, which accounts for the average being somewhat below the common standard. All men are set down as "drinking" who are not conscientiously opposed to the use of ardent spirit in *any form* and *under all circumstances*, as a beverage :

"Of ninety-eight warrant officers and privates, in politics sixty-five were straight Republicans, fourteen conservative Republicans, and three radical Republicans; eleven Union, three Democrats, one Abolitionist, and one undecided.

Thirty-two worship at the Unitarian Church, twenty-one at the Congregationalist, nineteen at the Methodist, fourteen at the Episcopal, eight at the Baptist, and four at the Universalist. Thirty-four are communicants of churches as follows: fourteen of the Methodist church, seven of the Congregational, five of the Episcopal, three of the Unitarian, three of the Baptist, and two of the Universalist.

The average age of the company is thirty-two years seven and seventeen forty-ninths days. The youngest man is seventeen years old, and the oldest forty.

The average height is five feet seven and nine-one hundred and ninety-sixths inches. The shortest man is five feet three and one-quarter inches, the tallest six feet one and one-quarter inches.

The average weight of the company is one hundred and thirty-seven and seventeen forty-ninth pounds. The heaviest man weighs one hundred and sixty-five pounds, the lightest one hundred and fifteen pounds.

Forty-four are set down as drinking; seven as drinking nothing stronger than cider and ale; and forty-seven as not drinking ardent spirits in any shape.

Fifty-seven smoke and forty-four do not; twenty-three neither drink nor smoke; thirty-three both drink and smoke; twenty-four smoke, but do not drink; and eighteen drink, but do not smoke.

There are nine married men and three widowers in the company, and sixteen admit that they are engaged to be married.

The occupations of the company, present and prospective, are as follows:

Thirty-seven intend to be or are merchants; four clergymen, eight lawyers, five farmers, four "literateurs," two physicians, two engineers, two printers, two cabinet makers, two machinists, two musicians, and one of each of the following: chemist, soldier, boot and shoe maker, manufacturer, provision dealer, banker, marble-worker, blacksmith, sailmaker, tea-broker, baker, druggist, expressman, jeweler, salesman, bookkeeper; ten are undecided.

There are in the company sixteen graduates and undergraduates, all from Harvard.

The close of another week still finds us

> " Down by the Readville farm,"

and, with the exception of yesterday and to-day, a glorious week we have had; choice October days, such as call

> ——" the squirrel and the bee
> From out their woodland home."

Indian Summer days, fit to inspire poetry in minds most prosaic: a warm sun, an empurpled atmosphere, soft breathing winds, and painted forests to feed the eye withal; glorious moon-lit nights and music to invite visitors: to render charming the duties of the sentinel, " pacing his lonely beat," and to render a healthy life altogether beautiful. A late sunset afforded a spectacle gorgeous as a dream of fairy land. As such a cloud-scene occurs no more than once or twice in a life-time, I cannot forbear to mention the magnificent assembling and coloring of clouds which waited upon the retiring day-king on Tuesday, and impressed every beholder with something of celestial beauty. To live in the midst of such scenes and such surroundings are among the soldier's recompenses. Happy for the soldier if he retains the power to enjoy them!

Wednesday afternoon and evening brought us a host of visitors. The rumors of our near departure brought a perfect cloud of friends. The evening was magnificent, and the tide of social enjoyment ran high. The band discoursed its best music, and our company glee clubs filled the interims quite acceptably. Our leading singers have a large repertory of fine sentimental songs, in addition to a large number of improvisations based upon the " Fourth Battalion" chorus, which runs in this wise:—

> " Fourth Battalion, 'talion,
> Fourth Battalion, 'talion,
> Fourth Battalion,
> Down by the Bigelow farm."

The novelty of our diet has suggested such parodies as the following:

> " Ham for breakfast, breakfast,
> Ham for breakfast, breakfast,
> Ham for breakfast,
> Down by the Readville farm.
>
> Ham for dinner, dinner,
> Ham for dinner, dinner,
> Ham for dinner,
> Down by the Readville farm."

And so on for supper.  Then again the chorus is varied by substituting the word rice for ham, and with equal effect.  Military lessons are sometimes conveyed in the same air, as follows:

> " Keep your butts back, butts back,
> Keep your butts back, butts back,
> Keep your butts back,
> Down by the Readville farm."

Then again :

> " Thir-teen inches, inches,
> Thir-teen inches, inches,
> Thir-teen inches,
> From breast to back."

Another favorite route-step song is known as " Saw my leg off," set to an old devotional air, and comprised in these four words, frequently repeated, with the addition of the word "*short*," pronounced in the most abrupt and explosive manner of which human lungs are capable.  The effect is rather sublime, as may be imagined.

On Thursday we were treated to a magnificent march over Brush Hill—our first brush.  Every inch of the route, which carried us over the most beautiful portion of Milton, and past the residences of the Forbeses, was picturesque as the dream of a poet.  Let those who may think this comparison overwrought, pursue the same route one of these fine October days, and then pause to catch the view of sea and landscape from Milton Hill.  Our march, which included a distance of fourteen miles, was, considering the state of the atmosphere, the severest of our experience ; but it was cheered by the smiles and waving handkerchiefs of beautiful women in windows, gateways, balconies, and groves; and by their more substantial favors in the shape of apples, pears, and cool water.  The few men who fell out of the ranks from faintness and exhaustion were of the reputed tougher sort—men of out-door life and pursuits.  Your professional men and clerks, clean-limbed and elastic, are the men to endure hardships, all the talk to the contrary notwithstanding.  This, I believe, was the observation of the " *Little* Corporal."

Among the late testimonials in the 44th deserving of mention, are the presentation of a knife, fork, and spoon, in a neat case, to each of the recruits from Framingham, by their friends in that town, and a sword, sash, belt, and various smaller articles of value and convenience, to Orderly Edmands, of Company A, by his friends in that company.

Your correspondent, and the other members of Company D, are indebted to Corporal Gardner for the introduction of a company dog—Romeo, a promising fellow, whose laughing countenance, waving tail, and general intelligence have already won him a host of friends. Several of the boys are industriously laboring to reconcile him to the society of a cat which has come to our barrack.

Mr. Burrage, of the firm of J. M. Beebe & Co., has presented to each member of Company C, Captain Lombard, one of Short's patent box knapsacks. If they can be manufactured in season to supply us before our departure South, the other members of the regiment will probably supply themselves with this knapsack at their own expense, which will amount to $2.50 per man. This knapsack is so adjusted to the shoulders as to be carried with much greater ease than the government article.

At this writing it is generally believed that we shall sail for Newbern about the middle of next week. For particular information on this point, and also with reference to state-rooms and sleeping cars, the public is directed to the Quartermaster's Department, where tickets for such like mythical accommodations are freely dispensed for satisfactory considerations.

By favor of private Geo. W. Sawin, I am this week enabled to give the following statistics of Company D, Captain Sullivan:

Clerks fifty-four, merchants five, farmers four, carpenters two, hotel keepers two, marble workers two, and one each of the following: astronomer, sailor, piano-forte tuner, civil engineer, architect, blacksmith, druggist, glass-blower, jeweller, shoe dealer, surveyor, clergyman, editor, machine stitcher, designer. Seven are under-graduates and one a graduate of Tufts College, one an under-graduate of Harvard and one of Yale. Ninety are single, seven married, and three " engaged." Thirty-three are Unitarians, thirty Universalists, thirteen Orthodox, ten Baptists, three Episcopalians, two Swedenborgians, one Presbyterian, one Methodist, four undecided. Five are church communicants.

Sixty-one are Republicans, and seven ask to be recorded as Abolitionists. The whole sixty-one sustain the emancipation proclamation. There is one " conservative " Republican, thirteen " Union " men, four Douglas Democrats, nine Democrats, and two undecided.

Forty-two do not drink distilled liquors, fifty-five do. The oldest man is aged thirty-three, the youngest eighteen. The average age is twenty-two and two ninety-sevenths. The average height, in shoes, is five feet nine and one-half inches. The tallest man is six feet one inch high; the shortest man five feet three inches. The heaviest man weighs one hundred and eighty-four pounds; the lightest one hundred and fifteen. The average weight is one hundred and forty-two-ninety-sevenths pounds.

---

In Barracks at Readville,
Saturday, Oct. 18, 1862.

When in my last I made allusion to our company dog Romeo and his feline companion, we could not foresee the sad and sudden rupture of all the relations between us. On Sunday a fiat from headquarters sent Romeo out of camp; the succeeding night pussy departed this life. Did she die of grief at the loss of Romeo? No one can say; but general opinion inclines to catalepsy. Her little stiffened body was encoffined in a paper box, and placed in the centre of the barrack. A small American flag was thrown over it, and the boys gathering about the remains sung Pleyel's Hymn with an appearance of solemnity that was altogether irresistible. The remains were then carefully placed upon an extemporized bier, and borne to the rear of the kitchen in the midst of a formidable guard of honor, marching with arms reversed, and chanting doleful symphonies. The weeping skies were in sympathy with the occasion; and the clouds were soon shedding tears upon the turf imprisoning the pet of the barrack. Imaginary vollies were fired, but all was *not* over. The funeral party had no sooner returned to the barrack than rumors of foul play began to circulate. A horrid secret was believed to be involved in the death of the cat. Suspicion fell upon a man whose bunk she had lately occupied, and who had been heard to utter threats against pussy for certain alleged rank offenses. The suspected party was arrested, a court organized, the defendant tried, convicted, and sentenced to subsist two days upon the rations. The unhappy man, anticipating his fate, made .three desperate attempts to escape, but was foiled in each instance, and forced to submit to the decree of justice.

A large number of the regiment have submitted to vaccination. "Corporal" desires to acknowledge the neat and thorough manner in which our assistant surgeon, Dr. Fisher, performed the operation. As the necessity of severe sanitary discipline is becoming apparent to all, the fidelity of Dr. Ware and his assistant are regarded with more favor than at first.

The close resemblance between the life of a soldier in barrack and that of a State Prison convict, regarded in certain outward aspects, affords mingled amusement and disgust. We go for our rations in single file, and with tin mugs and plates. The intercourse between officers and subordinates is scarcely less reserved; and the punishment for small offenses scarcely less severe with the soldier than the prisoner. On inspection days we stand up like well-burnished automata, and are as sensitive to praise or censure regarding the condition of our quarters, guns, &c., as so many children. At our meals and in our bunks we are stared at by visitors just as I remember to have stared at the happy family of "Honorable Gideon Haynes," at Charlestown, on various occasions. When impelled by "sanitary reasons," our keen-eyed surgeons pass through the barracks to see that nothing contraband nestles in the bunks, that the blankets and overcoats are accurately folded, and that only a certain amount of clothing and baggage per man is retained, we stand about and gaze at them just as your readers will remember they were gazed at by the inmates of the House of Correction which they visited not long ago. On these occasions your correspondent amuses himself by imaginatively regarding private A., with wild hair, as a desperate burglar; private B., of retiring manners, as an incorrigible thief; private L., the gay Lothario, as a heartless deceiver and bigamist; hirsute private T., smoking the inevitable briarwood, as a notorious but chivalric foot-pad; privates F., S., &c., of auburn hair, as the persistent incendiaries; and so on.

More princely donations have been made to some of the companies of the 44th regiment. To Co. C, Captain Richardson, Wm. Cumston, Esq., of the firm of Hallett & Cumston, has presented a check for five hundred dollars.

To the same company donations amounting to three hundred dollars, for the purchase of the improved knapsack, have been made by the following gentlemen:

J. M. Beebe & Co., F. Skinner & Co., Alexander Beal, C. W. Cartwright, W. P. Sargent, J. R. Tibbets, Read, Gardner & Co., Wilkinson, Stetson & Co., J. C. Converse & Co., E. & F. King & Co., Horatio Harris, Gorham Rogers.

To Co. H, Captain Smith, C. F. Hovey & Co. have presented a full set of the patent knapsacks. Co. K, Captain Reynolds, have been favored in the same way by a number of friends of that company, and Captain Reynolds has received from the men of his company the gift of a splendid sword. Co. F, Captain Storrow, have received the present of a set of patent knapsacks. The generous donor is too modest to let his name be known, but it is surmised that a young corporal of Co. F knows all about it.

The wife of Col. Lee has kindly remembered each soldier of the regiment by the gift of a little testimonial card, upon one side of which is printed the Old Hundreth Psalm, and upon the other the name of the recipient written in a neat hand.

On Wednesday we were visited by Governor Andrew and his military family. We received His Excellency with all the honors, and then marched in review. It is believed that better marching and wheelings than those exhibited by the 44th regiment on this occasion have rarely been witnessed by Governor Andrew or any other Governor.

I believe the Governor was accompanied by some members of the Sanitary Commission; but the investigations of that body of gentlemen were nearly confined to the *cuisine* at headquarters. They certainly couldn't be expected to labor upon empty stomachs; but when they had satisfied their hunger, it was too late to see the barracks by day-light. We shall accept the omission as a mark of confidence in the cleanliness and good order of this regiment.

We have had a good share of dismal weather the past week, and have not been allowed the consolation of smoking in the barracks; but the boys have managed to keep the blue devils at bay with mock parades and shows of great effectiveness. One day the camp was electrified by the appearance of an exceedingly well got up elephant, not unprovided with a tail, and waving a trunk of twisted shoddy. Another day we were visited by citizens of Brobdignag, ten feet high in their stockings.

Yesterday we made a march of twelve miles through West Roxbury and Dedham. On the way we caught a dim and fleeting glimpse of dear old Boston rising beyond a succession of tree-crowned hills. I remember the scene as a beautiful phantasmagoria, such as will come to us in dreams while we encamp upon Southern soil. The march was less delightful than that to Milton Hill. The day was murky, and the air lifeless. There was little to impart zest to the exercise. Sunlight is as important for out-door physical enjoyment as fresh air, and a soldier makes a mistake in choosing a cloudy day for a march.

We now expect to remain at Readville till the close of the war, except in case Readville is invaded by the enemy, when we shall make a masterly retreat to Mill Village.

To protect us against the strong winds of the inclement season approaching, as well as to impart an air of sylvan beauty to the camp, a dense grove of pine saplings has been planted a little to the South of the barracks. Great praise is due to Lieut. Stebbins, our unwearied chief of police this week, for the well-considered arrangement of this great work.

---

In the Cars, Wednesday Morning, &rbrace;
Oct. 22, 1862. &rbrace;

I have just time during our run into Boston this morning to say "good bye" to your readers until we arrive at Newbern, N. C. After seven weeks and a half of barrack life at Readville, we at last find ourselves en route for Dixie. To the experience of these seven weeks and a half we shall doubtless many times revert as the poetry of our military experience. There was no little heart in the cheers we gave for the "old camp" as we stood for the last time in the company streets. The old camp at Readville is fraught with pleasant memories of soldierly discipline, of the faithfulness and kindness of our officers, of genial companionship, and a thousand incommunicable pleasures of social life, multiplied and enhanced by the visits and offerings of hosts of friends from Boston and elsewhere.

At our dress parades last evening, after devotional services, our Colonel met a response in the heart of every man in his regiment when he called for three times three for the "good old State and the dear ones we leave behind us." The cheers were given with emphasis; and so were nine others for Col. Lee. "Boys," said the Colonel in response, I know you meant those cheers for *all* your officers. Whatever may be your fortune hereafter, rest assured we shall stand by you. Let us all perform our duty to the State and the United States, and may God help us all!" The emotion exhibited by Col. Lee was communicated through the regiment, and there were many wet eyes among soldiers and spectators as we marched back to the barracks.

As soon as practicable, I shall resume this correspondence, confident that it will find readers among the many friends of the 44th in Boston.

---

On Board Transport Steamer Merrimac, &rbrace;
Oct. 23, 1862. &rbrace;

We lay off Deer Island the night of our embarkation, (last night) and about six o'clock this morning weighed anchor. It was pleasant to sleep one night more so near to dear old Boston, where we knew so many hearts were throbbing at the thought of us. The thousands of lights which came to us in a semi-circle from over the water, seemed like the steady beaming of so many loving eyes, and may be our dreams were the sweeter for the fancy. Don't imagine, however, that we all slept as quietly as we did in those luxurious bunks at Readville. The 44th Regiment occupies the lower deck of the Merrimac, and has already had a decided flavor of life in the steerage. Here we are, "the flower" (or flour) " of the youth of Boston," (*vide* Boston Journal of October 23,) packed like so many herrings in the steerage. Our bunks are not half as good as those at Readville, and, sad to say, we haven't enough even of these. They afford us little more than space enough in which to turn over. Here and there we are afforded a small glimmer of light from the deck, and a little fresh air by devious channels. Into the bunk of your correspondent it happens to come in an unpleasantly strong current, as if to rebuke his former passionate professions of love for fresh air under more favorable circumstances, or as a piece of retributive justice for opening doors and windows against the protests of tender comrades.

The five hundred men of the Third Regiment who accompany us, and who are known by their black overcoats as the " men in mourning," are better commoded between decks, one story above us. They will do, but as for ourselves, as we lie stretched out here in this dark, reptile sort of existence, we are fain to ask ourselves if we are really intelligent beings with souls; if the "flower" has really come to this; if the " pet of many a household," (*vide* Boston Transcript of Oct. 22) has really been reduced to treatment no better than that of the poorest emigrant. But we ought not to grumble while scores of our regiment are obliged to stretch themselves upon the cold deck, upon the hatches, passage ways, &c. ; and we do *not* grumble. Your correspondent only gives *facts*. He, like many others, *expected* to " rough it," and rather likes it.

Our breakfast this morning was a mug of very muddy coffee, and a piece of bread. For dinner we were afforded boiled beef and potatoes and coffee, but no bread. We could get along better with this but for occasional tantalizing sights and smells of poultry and puddings and garden vegetables which grace the cabin tables. Our officers confess that they live like fighting cocks, but they should have the credit of sincerely commiserating our unavoidable treatment. O, genial-hearted lobster-man of the rubicund face and Pickwickian aspect, who rose to bless us in Commercial street, could you but waft us one fish from your shelly store, we know how much good it would do you and us ; but tonight, alas, we were forced to sup on bread and water, with a dessert of aggravating conversation about porter house steaks, cold chicken, warm biscuit, etc., etc. If we live we will have our revenge some day at Parker's goodly hostelry.

FRIDAY, OCT. 24.

It is said that we made sixteen miles an hour last night, running ninety-six miles in six hours. We have passed Montauk Light, and at this writing (between eight and nine o'clock) we are supposed to be somewhere off the Jersey shore. Our consort, the Mississippi, has been in sight over our starboard quarter all the morning. Thus far the weather has been extremely favorable, but we have not all escaped the misery of sea-sickness—a malady which must have been aggravated by our close, ill-ventilated quarters, and the unavoidable filth attending the herding together of fifteen hundred men on shipboard. Scarcely a breath of air was stirring last night, and very little came down to our bunks. After remaining on deck a few moments this morning, an attempt to penetrate to our quarters induced a nausea which we found impossible to endure, and so we incontinently rushed upon deck to swallow our rations, without the intervention of spoon or plate. We were first served to a large piece of bread and a mug of coffee, and then to parboiled rice, which rattled upon our plates. O, Readville rations, bad as you might have been, may the tongue that utters aught against you cleave to the roof of the slanderer's mouth. It is expected we are to have beef for dinner, as several noble quarters were not long since dragged along close by the rear of the horses' stalls, on their way to the boilers, where they were set to cooking without washing.

We wish our friends could see us at meal times. We are a study for an artist at those interesting periods. We are obliged to eat on the upper deck. One fellow is seen burying his nose in a loaf of bread, another gnaws a beef bone until his face is resplendant with grease ; but the colored boy of the color company, making his dinner from a mass of fat and gristle, is the observed of all observers. His face shines like varnished ebony, but he is still intent upon his greasy repast, and oblivious to the smiles and jeers of the amused spectators who surround him. Feed away, juvenile Ethiop, woolly headed Mark Tapley, may nothing come between you and jolliness forever.

This afternoon we were signalled by the Mississippi, when she came up to within hailing distance. Hearty cheers were exchanged between the swarms on the decks of either steamer. We were glad to notice on board the Mississippi one lieutenant and a number of non-coms. whom the Merrimac had unfortunately left behind. As night shuts in we are supposed to be off Fortress Monroe. We have a balmy atmosphere and a brisk wind from the west. Hundreds of the boys have stretched themselves for sleep upon the upper deck.

SATURDAY, Oct. 25.

This morning we are supposed to be steaming along between Fortress Monroe and Cape Hatteras. The sea is smooth, and the genial breath of the South is upon us. We feel as if Spring-time had come upon us suddenly, and those not afflicted with sea-sickness feel good this morning. The Mississippi is just ahead of us.

On board these two steamers are three thousand soldiers with arms and accoutrements. We are the same as defenceless. From our vast navy of war vessels not even one little gunboat has been spared to escort us to our destination, and this in the face and eyes of the fact that a number of formidable rebel privateers are scouring the seas and scattering destruction in their path. Is there any apology for such risk and negligence? We cannot see it.

As the weather becomes soft, genial and glorious upon deck, our situation below grows more intolerable. It is almost impossible to exaggerate the uncomfortable, unhealthy character of our quarters upon the lower deck. A prison dungeon is not worse supplied with air and sunlight; and to make matters still worse, the ship has but a miserable supply of lanterns at night. It is to be acknowledged that there are a few feeble devices for sending air below, but they are altogether inadequate. With the splendid machinery on board this steamer, it would be an easy matter by the use of fans to thoroughly ventilate every portion of the ship. In the course of another century, ship-builders will learn, as house-builders are now learning, that means must be employed for the introduction of a plenty of fresh air into all structures where men are herded together. We cannot be too thankful that the weather has been so favorable since we left Boston. A thousand sick men in such quarters as these would have made a hell afloat. Now I would like to speak a good word for the ship. She is staunch, steady, swift and well officered. She has carried twenty-three hundred men, but only a thousand and comfort can dwell together upon her decks. The few who get a chance to wash their hands and faces are obliged to do so in salt water. It is reported that Capt. Sampson was quite thunderstruck by a request of our officers that he would afford us means of daily ablutions, and that he remarked we were the first regiment he ever carried who had expressed a desire to wash their hands and faces.

Our "holy friars," the black-coated men of the 3d regiment, appear to be a good set of fellows, and we all get along most amicably together. Col. Richmond and Major Morrissey accompany this half of the regiment.

We have been thoughtfully regaled with an apple apiece a day, and they have proved wonderfully refreshing, especially as we are allowed but two meals a day on shipboard. Now, when we most need a sutler, no sutler is to be seen, although at rare intervals we can buy hard apples at five cents apiece, and cake at fifty cents a pound. Last evening Co. F were regaled with a dish of tea by some Good Samaritan, said to be Capt. Storrow, who is highly praised for his careful attention to the men of his command. I wish to bear similar testimony in behalf of the officers of Co. D, Capt. Sullivan and Lieuts. Blake and Stebbins.

I wish my fun-loving readers could have stood at the hatchway between decks this morning, and seen the soldiers slide down the slippery stairs. Some carried mugs of coffee with no other apparent object than to pour the beverage upon the heads and shoulders of those who preceded them. The libation was not greatly enjoyed except by a crowd of spectators at the foot of the stairs, who hailed every accident and discomfiture of the sort with shouts of laughter.

SUNDAY MORNING, OCT. 26.

At 9 o'clock this morning we are in near view of the North Carolina coast, and doubtless very near Beaufort. Last night, like all the weather during the voyage, was delightful, and the long upper deck was literally packed with sleepers lying at every possible angle and posture, with arms and legs affectionately crossed and interlocked. The general health of the men remains excellent.

Eleven o'clock finds us at the wharf at Morehead City, near Beaufort, and making preparations for a speedy landing in the midst of a drizzling rain.

This letter is written without conveniences, and under the most miserable and disagreeable circumstances.

We are soon to take the cars for Newbern. You will hear from me there.

———

NEWBERN, N. C., OCT. 26, 1862.

When we stepped from the decks of the Merrimac we were provided with shelter from a drizzling rain in the depot of the railroad connecting Morehead with Newbern; and while there we made the structure ring with patriotic and devotional songs—our first salute to Dixie. We were conveyed from Morehead to Newbern on platform cars, and were, of course, entirely exposed to the weather. We had scarcely got under way before there set in a violent rain, which continued almost without intermission until our arrival at Newbern. Our garments, of course, were thoroughly drenched, but, nevertheless, the trip was highly enjoyed. The mild and invigoring pine breezes of the old North State contrasted so deliciously with the foetid atmosphere and filth of the steamer, that even a drenching rain was insufficient to quench our exhilaration of spirits. A more miserable and worthless tract of country than the barren pine region which we traversed cannot well be imagined, so that under all the circumstances of the trip, our lively frame of mind may be regarded as quite Mark Tapleyish. Pickets from the Massachusetts 27th regiment were scattered along the road at frequent intervals. We cheered them, and they cheered us. Some of them were sheltered by tents, others in cabins, and some in substantial log structures calculated for defence. Occasional negro villages, and scattering negro huts were objects of lively interest. All hands turned out to see us as we shot past. The men showed their entire ivory, and the women threw their black arms up and down in the most vehement approbation. We also witnessed several good specimens of the real Southern " white trash." The country is well calculated to develop this species of the genus homo. The women are the most doleful and disgusting looking of their sex. We suspected all of them of looking secesh daggers at us. A few did cheer us on after a fashion, waving their arms up and down—a sort of melancholy God-speed. We doubt if they possessed a solitary white handkerchief, or any other white textile fabric proper to be displayed on such occasions. We once stopped to water the iron horse close by a field of sweet potatoes growing within some rebel breastworks erected to command the railroad. The proprietor of the potato patch came forth with his wife and children and presented us several handsful of the vegetables, for which they were rewarded with vociferous cheers as the train rolled on.

At dusk we crossed the river Neuse, and found ourselves in the pretty little city of Newbern, where, as may be guessed, we received a hearty welcome from the Massachusetts men stationed at this place. Our friends, the contrabands, were not the least enthusiastic of those who welcomed us. We were quartered for the night in a spacious machine shop, well lighted with gas. We have just supped upon hard bread and codfish broiled upon a forge. An attempt was made to supply us with coffee, but it miserably failed, and your correspondent is one of a respectable number who go to bed without the soldier's chiefest bodily consolation. As he closes his record of the day the air in the machine shop is thick with hard bread and flying codfish sent from invisible hands.

October 27, 1862.

Our men are scattered about town this morning, luxuriating upon such breakfasts as can be purchased with money. They are constantly coming in with beaming faces and tantalizing narrations of what they got to eat. Your correspondent only strayed a few steps from the engine house before he found a little cabin where a neat colored woman served him with two kinds of hoe-cake, roasted sweet potatoes, and sage tea.

We have not been in Newbern long enough to give you much news. Barracks are erecting here, it is reported, for fifteen thousand soldiers. Ours are not yet completed. Among the regiments at Newbern and vicinity are the Massachusetts 17th, 23d, 24th, 25th, 27th, and 44th. The 3d and 5th which were detained at Morehead City by the grounding of the Mississippi, will probably arrive here to-day.

---

NEWBERN, N. C., WEDNESDAY, OCT. 29, 1862.

We are encamped upon the western bank of the river Neuse, about one-third of a mile to the north of the city of Newbern. Monday night most of the regiment passed in tents, a few rods from here. Yesterday we were industriously employed in ditching and smoothing the ground around our cloth-houses, laying floors, constructing fire places and chimneys, and had just got things in the most satisfactory condition, when Company D was ordered to strike tents and go into the half-completed barrack which we now occupy conjointly with the carpenters and a great quantity of loose lumber. In a very short time all our companies will be comfortably housed, unless unexpected orders intervene. The barracks of each regiment are continuous—occupying one long building. They are provided with windows and more commodious bunks than those at Readville. Our easterly windows look out upon the Neuse. On the other side the barrack is shaded with cedar trees. To the west of us is encamped the Connecticut Tenth Regiment, a Rhode Island Battery, and the New York Third Artillery Regiment. A New York cavalry regiment is also encamped in the vicinity. These are all additional to the troops in this department mentioned in my last letter.

The Connecticut Tenth, although much reduced in numbers and effectiveness, has greatly surprised us new comers by the excellency of their manual drill.  It is almost equal to that of the Chicago Zouaves.

The men of the old regiments at Newbern are not inclined to regard the nine months' men with much favor, and indulge in a good many taunts having reference to bounty money and good clothes.  They take great pleasure in assuring us that General Foster proposes to give us a full nine months' *work*, and that we need not expect to escape the warmest part of the business before us.  They are considerably disgusted with our unveteran-like ways, and furnish us with innumerable suggestions.  The bugles, numbers, &c., upon our caps, they regard as vanity.  They allow no " cullured pusson " to wear Uncle Sam's buttons, and it is now rumored that those of our boys who shall appear in the streets of Newbern with " infantry " buttons will find themselves suddenly minus those articles.  The soldier who returns the salute of a negro is set down as a transgressor of military etiquette, and privates who salute each other are laughed at.

The remarks of one of our boys that " there is nothing but niggers and soldiers in Newbern," well describes the impression of your correspondent.  Most of the resident secesh skedaddled long ago, and as others become unearthed, and refuse to take the oath, they are conveyed beyond the Union lines.  Many white residents, professedly Union, are believed to be playing possum.

The first night we spent in Newbern is said to have been the coldest of the season up to that time.  Monday night and Tuesday morning also seemed very much like late October days in New England, and required about the same number of woollen blankets and overcoats as are requisite at home now-a-days.  We are cautioned to be out but little in the evening, and to wear overcoats after five o'clock.  We are also very earnestly cautioned to drink but little water, and to eat sparingly of negro " chicken fixins " in the shape of sweet potatoes, pies and cakes, which contrabands bring into camp in great profusion.

We are no sooner comfortably settled in barracks than word comes to us of an immediate march into the interior of the State, perhaps to Kinston, perhaps to Swansbororough, which are in possession of the rebels.  At all events we are doubtless bound to extend our lines, and we now have the troops to do it with, although we scarcely expected that General Foster would put us in motion quite so speedily as this.

The health of the regiment is excellent, everything considered.

Lieutenant Blake, of Company D, has been detailed to act upon the staff of Colonel Stevenson, commanding our brigade. We thus lose an invaluable officer from our company. Lieutenant Stebbins, who succeeds Lieut. Blake, is one of the most faithful and considerate officers in the regiment, and will make the place of Lieutenant Blake good.

---

WASHINGTON, N. C., OCT. 31, 1862.

As remarked in my last letter from Newbern, we had no sooner got comfortably ensconced in our splendid new barracks than we received orders to join one of the largest military expeditions which has been known in North Carolina for many a day. The expedition consists of nearly all the available force at Newbern and vicinity, infantry, artillery and cavalry, and cannot fall much below ten thousand men, most of whom left Newbern early yesterday morning, on board steam transports, and schooners propelled by tugs, under the command of Major-General Foster.

We were in what is called light marching order: but our two blankets, haversacks containing three days' rations of hard bread, beef, coffee and sugar, canteens, equipments and rifles, made up a very considerable load.

After about thirty hours of slow steaming down the Neuse, through Pamlico Sound and up the Tar river, we disembarked at Washington, one of the bastard " cities " of North Carolina. A journey more tame in its surroundings can scarcely be imagined. The shores of the two rivers present an almost unbroken level; and the monotony of a stunted growth of trees is barely interrupted by the habitations of man. In places the trees have a beautiful coloring, which reminded us of the October woods in New England, and there is a sort of lonesome grandeur in the broad streams themselves.

Washington looks like Newbern. Some of the streets are prettily shaded, and there are a few elegant residences. At a window of one of the latter we espied a pretty young white woman playing a piano. Besides these, having been here only a couple of hours or so, I saw little but " niggers and soldiers," a phrase which also describes Newbern. We were marched through the town into a breezy field on the shore of the Tar river, where we stacked arms, made fires, and boiled our coffee. Finding ourselves in the vicinity of a row of negro shanties, the board fences surrounding them were soon converted into fuel and shelter. The shanties were then besieged by our hungry boys, and the black "aunties" and their daughters were soon driving a good business in supplying the soldiers with hoe-cake.

The vociferous demands of the boys to be supplied in their turn were quite confusing to the accommodating cooks, who mixed their meal and water and transferred it to iron pans with the rapidity of experts in the business. Each fire-place was surrounded by hungry expectants, some of whom, to make sure of their cakes, drew their initials in the yielding dough, and then stood by like watch-dogs until the tempting morsel was browned and "soaked" to the point of perfection. "Soaked" is a word of the cook, and describes the finishing process. The venerable proprietor of one of the shanties remarked that he was glad to see the Yankees, but this was the second time they had torn down his fence.

Washington is reputed to be a "Union city." In the language of one of the inhabitants, "There was a right smart of Union here before the proclamation, but now it is the other way." It's of no consequence, as Toots says. The North Carolina First Regiment is here.

EVENING.—We bivouac to-night upon the northerly shore of the Tar River. The field is covered with extemporized shelters of rude but ingenious construction, and are supplied with generous beds of corn-husks. Some sugar-box shooks in the vicinity have been levied upon, and some of the boys are literally boxing themselves up. Others have stretched their rubber blankets for shelter. Some have constructed shanties of boards. Our woollen blankets have been voted an incumbrance, and are packed away. For the lively work now in prospect we must per force carry lighter loads than we brought from Newbern; and although we shall miss the blankets o' nights, we shall miss them more upon our wearisome marches when every ounce weighs a pound.

I cannot tell you what we are going to do. There is supposed to be work enough, especially as it is reported that fifteen thousand rebel troops are in North Carolina, and some of them at no great distance from this point. We may next be heard from at Kinston or Williamston.

---

ON BOARD TRANSPORT STEAMER GEO. COLLINS,  ⎫
FROM PLYMOUTH TO NEWBERN, N. C.                ⎬
TUESDAY, NOV. 11, 1862.  ⎭

Your correspondent finds himself one of a large expeditionary corps en route back to Newbern, after one of the longest and severest marches in the history of the present war. Since the date of my last,

which was written at Washington, at the head of Pamlico Sound, the
regiment has led rather an active and stirring life for a regiment only
about sixty days old. We left Washington early Sunday morning,
Nov. 2d, marching northward that day nearly twenty miles, with nothing to break the monotony save a light brush with the enemy's picket
a few miles out of town. We bagged one or two of their horses, and
soon passed their bivouac, where a rebel blanket and some other articles were burning. Here the road forked, and upon the left the smoke
of a burning bridge showed that the rebels were making good their
escape. At noon we halted near the plantation of a decently to-do
farmer. A son of the farmer was observed to wear rebel buttons, and
he was taken prisoner. There was then little doubt as to the rebel
proclivities of the old man (a good tow-headed, blear-eyed specimen of
white trash,) whose premises were pretty thoroughly searched for the
means of providing dinner and other refreshments. Sweet potatoes,
apple brandy, honey, &c., helped the boys' rations amazingly, and
these delicacies were relished the more because they were taken along
with several rebel weapons of death. The female portion of the family
sat upon the piazza and gazed upon the soldiers with a sort of stolid
fear depicted upon their faces. They were tolerably good looking, and
one of them wore a quiet, venerable aspect, which moved our respect
and sympathy. At dusk we stirred up a secesh hornets' nest, and a
lively battle of musketry was heard in front. As we hurried forward
Gen. Foster sat with his staff at a bend in the road, and smilingly informed us that there were " only seven or eight hundred of them."
Just before this our two right flank companies, H and C, Capts. Smith
and Lombard, were detached from the regiment and sent forward as
skirmishers.

Proceeding by the road they descended a hill and entered a piece of
woods through which ran a considerable stream of water. They had
no sooner entered the water at the fording-place than they were fired
upon by a considerable force of rebel infantry in ambuscade; but our
men bravely stood their ground, and replied promptly to the fire.
After a few rounds, the guns and ammunition became useless from wet-
ting, when companies H and C were withdrawn, although not until they
had crossed the ford. Companies E and I, Captains Spencer Richardson
and Kendall, were sent forward. Company I was held in reserve, while
E succeeded in passing the ford and ascended to the summit of a hill
on the opposite side, but not without brisk skirmishing, receiving and
returning several volleys, and capturing three prisoners. One of these

was taken by private Michael Parsons under circumstances so creditable to his pluck that Parsons was promoted to a sergeantcy.

After Company E, the stream was crossed by the Connecticut 10th regiment, Colonel Pettiborn. The ford being thus thoroughly commanded, word was sent to the rear, and the entire column moved forward, the 44th regiment passing the Connecticut 10th, thus giving to the Massachusetts 44th the honor of the next advance. Having attained the summit of the hill previously occupied by Company E. the 44th deployed on either side of the road, and allowed the Massachusetts 24th to pass to the front. The advance was again resumed, and we entered a piece of dense woods. Here we felt our way cautiously, once halting for a considerable space of time. The moon shone brightly, scattering the light through the scarcely moving branches. The voices of birds and the hum of insects filled the air with tones eloquent of summer at the North. The world looked too beautiful for strife and slaughter. Here we sunk down upon the ground, almost overcome by the fatigue of a day's severe march, and were with difficulty restrained from falling into a deep sleep. We were soon aroused by the order to advance, and proceeded cautiously about half a mile farther, the road skirting, for a portion of the distance, an open field on our left. Just at the extremity of this field we were again fired upon from the hedge. This hazardous kind of advancing was then wisely abandoned, and the column filed into the field, under the cover of Belger's splendid artillery, which having assumed a commanding position, shelled the rebel ambuscade in magnificent style. Sweeter music than the music of *those* spheres, whistling their way into the nest of cowardly traitors, never fell upon mortal ears. From our observation of the rapid and well-directed fire, we were not surprised to hear, as we did subsequently, that many a rebel bit the dust on the morning of the third of November, at "Chopper's Creek, near Rawle's Mill," which will stand for the name of this affair.

At the ford the casualities of the 44th consisted of the following :

Company E. Killed — Charles Morse. Wounded — Charles E. Roberts.

Company C. Killed — Charles Rollins. Slightly wounded — Sergeant Pond, William A. Smallidge. Lieutenant Briggs was momentarily stunned by the near passing of a projectile, but speedily recovered.

Company H. Killed — none. Wounded — Richard V. Depeyster, left arm amputated ; Jacobs, of South Scituate, in the back (severe) : Harrison Parker, 2d, in right arm (slightly).

At the place where we were last fired on, Lieutenant Stebbins, of Company D, while assisting in rallying the men of his company, was slightly wounded in one of his legs, and had his garments perforated in several places.

It is doubtful if the history of the war furnishes an instance where a skirmish with the enemy has occurred under circumstances more trying to the Union troops, or better calculated to test their moral endurance and pluck. A regiment only sixty days old altogether, without experience in battle, was called upon at the close of a day's severe march to encounter a deadly foe in ambuscade, upon ground of their own selection, at a long, deep ford, and in dense, dark woods; but I am happy to record the testimony of all observers that the officers and men of the 44th Regiment exhibited a gallantry and fearlessness befitting veterans themselves, and sufficient to gain expressions of admiration from the old regiments in the expedition, who had previously regarded us with, to draw it mildly, an over-critical eye, regarding us as more ornamental than useful.

Some of the last companies of the 44th to cross the ford were for several minutes under the fire of two rebel cannon planted on an eminence to our right. Grape and shell fell on either side of us in a lively manner, but, most fortunately, without injury to us. Before entering the ford a shower of bullets passed close over our heads as we lay in the road. Our recumbent position at this point, as well as at the last place of attack, doubtless saved us from considerable loss of life.

It was two hours past midnight before we received orders to bivouac, when we sunk down and slept upon our arms in the open air. It was a cold, damp night, and after a few hours' sleep, we awoke wet, cold and stiff, the combined effects of half an hour's bath in the stream the previous night, a heavy North Carolina dew, and the fatigue of the former day's march. When we opened our eyes we discovered that the field was traversed by a formidable rebel earthwork, of which our rapid advance had prevented the completion.

At an early hour Monday morning the column resumed its forward movement, and reached Williamston, a pretty town on the Roanoke river, where we were glad to find several of our gunboats and a lot of extra rations for our troops. Here we rested, foraged, dined and made ourselves extremely comfortable for a couple of hours or so. The white residents had skedaddled, and we entered into possession of their horses, mules, wagons, pigs, poultry and honey. From Williamston we advanced about five miles and bivouaced in a cornfield. On our route thither we were delayed two hours by the destruction of a bridge. Tuesday we dined at Hamilton, another town on the Roanoke, about the size of Williamston, where we again fared luxuriously upon the products of the country. In the evening we advanced beyond Hamilton about three miles, and encamped again in a corn-field. I regret to say that we left Hamilton by the light of several burning houses, which were said to have been fired by some soldiers in retaliation for the shooting of a Union soldier by a rebel picket near the town. The firing of the buildings was generally condemned as unnecessary and outrageous.

Wednesday, after a further advance of about a dozen miles, we halted for dinner upon the road to Tarboro'. After dinner we retraced our steps a couple of miles, and took a road to the right in the direction of Halifax, which we pursued until midnight through a miserable swampy territory before we found a place fit for an encampment. Here we bivouaced in rain and mud within six or seven miles of Tarboro', a reputed rebel stronghold having railroad communication with Weldon and Richmond. When we arose Thursday morning we were confidently expecting to march upon Tarboro', and were not a little surprised to find ourselves turning backward. Then came rumors thick and fast of a largely augmented rebel force at Tarboro', and of a design to cut off our retreat at the swamp in the event of our retreat.

When the columns changed roads on Wednesday, two companies of our regiment, A and G, Captains James Richardson and Hunt, together with two pieces of cannon and a small force of cavalry, all under the command of the Major of the New York 3d cavalry, were sent forward upon the direct route for the purpose, as it is supposed, of diverting the attention of the rebels from a proposed attack in the rear. The plan, however, if such was the plan, did not succeed. The little force soon found itself opposed to a formidable enemy in ambuscade, and after a somewhat brisk skirmish, in which one of our mounted pickets was killed, concluded it would be wise to rejoin our main force, which they did the next morning at day-light, at our encampment, after a forced and very fatiguing march, and, for a portion of the distance, upon the double quick.

Whatever may have been the truth regarding the rebel force in our vicinity, certain it is that we made a very rapid march back to Hamilton —a march which tested the endurance of our troops in no small degree —the more because of the uncomfortable weather and muddy condition

of the roads.  Never was the shelter of real houses more welcome than
to our jaded troops when they arrived at Hamilton on Thursday night.
We entered into possession of the deserted buildings, and were soon
basking in the genial warmth streaming from a hundred fire-places—
a warmth mingled with the savory odors of cooking meats and vegetables.  Some of the companies fell upon quarters almost luxurious.  All
were thankful for any kind of shelter.  In the morning we were a little
surprised to find the ground white with snow, and conjectured that the
" Sunny South" was ahead of Masachusetts in that particular, for once.

On Friday we marched to Williamston, where we tarried until Sunday morning, and recruited our strength by rest and comfortable fare.
Here we hoped to take transports for Newbern, but were destined for
one more day's march, and Sunday night we encamped near Plymouth,
after a quick march of nearly twenty miles.  Monday noon we embark-
ed for Newbern on board this steamer, having in tow a schooner with a
portion of the regiment.  We are in a gratified frame of mind.  Why
should we not be ?  We have succeeded in effecting a march of full one
hundred miles through the enemy's country ; we have been under fire,
and are said to have stood it in a creditable manner ; the endurance of
our troops has been tested as it never was before by the troops in North
Carolina, and a green regiment has been found as capable of performing
a severe march as the veterans of Roanoke and Newbern.  In fact few-
er men of the 44th fell out of the ranks from fatigue than those of any
other regiment in the three brigades composing the expedition.  It
must be confessed, however, that the old regiments do not give us any
extra credit for this endurance, but say we *ought* to march well, coming
as we do so recently from home, in good health, and before we have
been subjected to the hardships and sickness incident to the soldier.
There is, no doubt, much truth in this ; but it is almost a question
whether our advantages of condition are not offset by the seasoning and
experience of men a year in the field before us.  Moreover, and chiefly,
we have reason to feel satisfied with the expedition, forasmuch as Gen.
Foster says its object was accomplished.  What that object was is not
well known at this writing ; but it may have been the diversion of rebel
troops from Weldon, or Richmond, to aid General Dix on the one hand,
or General McClellan on the other.  We certainly succeeded in cleaning the rebel troops out of a large part of North Carolina, and in giving
them a terrible scare.

Our impressions of North Carolina have not been rendered more favorable by a more thorough acquaintance.  Most of the territory we

traversed is a dead, uninteresting level, thinly populated in times of peace, and almost depopulated by the war. We passed considerable growing cotton, and very many large fields of unharvested corn. We met a few white people, but scarcely a Union man or woman, even professedly. At Hamilton we found one gratifying exception in the person of a venerable man nearly eighty years of age, who welcomed us with emotion and bid us a regretful "good bye." He had a son in the rebel army—forced there by the conscription, after escaping three drafts. We sung several patriotic songs to the old man, who listened to us with uncovered head and streaming eyes, and bowed his grateful acknowledgements. There were few who witnessed the scene who did not share the old man's emotion. We left him with cheers and blessings, and felt our patriotism renewed by the interview.

Above Hamilton we passed a negro village, the residents of which assembled along the road to cheer us on. Their spokesman was an old colored man, who kept repeating, 'as the column passed along, *"We've long wished you well, but we daren't show it!"* This, too, was an inspiration to us, as was also the crowd of poor blacks following in our train wherever we moved, under a vague presentiment that the day of their redemption had come, and that liberty was in store for them.

Our friends will inquire as to what condition we find ourselves at the close of so severe a march. There are a few who have been placed upon the sick list in consequence of the severity of our experience, some of whom were sent to Newbern by gunboats from Hamilton when we first arrived there, and others to Plymouth by the same means, upon our return. There are many sore and bleeding feet which have worn out their shoes and stockings. Nearly all of us have lost several pounds of superfluous flesh, and some are quite gaunt and hirsute, not to say dirty. As a regiment, contrasted with our appearance at Readville, we may be said to look decidedly rough. Not a little of the "sacred soil" adheres to the late spotless blue of our habiliments. Grease spots and smut variegate our coats and pantaloons, which in some cases present large openings made by lying to closely to the camp fires. We would march twenty miles for the sake of exhibiting ourselves to our friends in Washington street as we look to-day.

A large army passing through an enemy's country presents a grand and formidable appearance to a novitiate like your correspondent, and it also presents features of a grotesque comicality scarcely less striking. As we advanced, our teams elongated with great rapidity. Every stray or deserted vehicle along our route, from a carryall to a handcart, and every horse and mule possessing the slightest power of locomotion, was pressed into our service. Some of the teams thus extemporised, and laden or driven by sick and disabled soldiers and contraband servants, would have done credit to any turn-out of the antiques and horribles. Some poor mules were literally covered with a burden of humanity equal to their own bulk. Many of our baggage wagons were drawn by mules, and at night their unmusical voices seemed raised in solemn protest against the hardships and abuse heaped upon their race.

Various instances of foraging, although not so funny to one party interested, were among the amusing episodes of our progress through North Carolina. It was not a little entertaining to see some of our boys, now in hot pursuit of half-frantic poultry and pigs, and then wildly beating the air in the vicinity of bee-hives which they had ruthlessly overturned in an irrepressible passion for stored sweets. The sight and taste of that white honey-comb will not soon pass from the memory of our jaded and hungry soldiers! Nor you, apple-jack, beverage of the South, cheering *and* inebriating, welcome substitute for whisky rations.

> " Here's to good old apple-jack,
> Drink her down ;
> Here's to good old apple-jack,
> Drink her down ;
> Here's to good old apple-jack,
> It will lay you on your back,
> Drink her down,
> Drink her down ! "

" Corporal " is not responsible for this. It was wafted to his ears from the quarter deck of the transport.

NEWBERN, Nov. 14, 1862.

We arrived here this morning. I had more to say, but have no time to say it before the close of the mail.

------

NEWBERN, N. C., Nov. 15, 1862.

By the last mail I sent you a hurried account of our recent expedition to the vicinity of Tarborough. Time was not afforded me to say all I desired to, nor all that would have been gratifying to the many friends of the 44th at home, who have to turn to the Herald for a connected account of our adventures.

What I wished to say in my previous letter, which, by the way, I hope escaped the Newbern censorship, and which I would say now, if it would not be unmilitary, was a word about one high in command in this regiment, who has more than met the sanguine expectations of those who knew him intimately as one apt to command, prompt in expedients, cool and collected in danger, tender-hearted to the sick and disabled, generous in all his promptings. The late trying experiences of the regiment enable me to speak unqualifiedly upon these points. It would also gratify your correspondent if he might be allowed to bear testimony to the high qualities of other field and staff officers, and to personally acknowledge the considerate kindness of those who had kind words and kinder acts for the sick, weary and foot-sore during our late severe march through the enemy's country. To one of our captains great praise is awarded for his unwavering endurance and pluck throughout the march ; the more as he had no sooner arrived at Washington, N. C., than he was deprived of his first Lieutenant, (detailed to act upon the staff of Colonel Stevenson, commanding our brigade,) and a day or two afterward, of his remaining Lieutenant, who was forced to return to Newbern in consequence of a wound received at the skirmish of Chopper's Creek. The manner in which the Captain alluded to, inexperienced in campaigning, and almost unaided, sustained his command, and kept his men together during the eight days' march, gave him a new hold upon the cordial respect of his company and superior officers.

You can suppose that we were glad to get back into comfortable barracks at Newbern, where we received a cordial and affectionate welcome from the Cripple Reserve and Home Guard, who had kept watch and ward over our knapsacks and made themselves comfortable, while we made eighteen miles a day and glory. But they wouldn't allow us to patronize them. *They* had seen service. Our pickets were driven in a night or two before, the long-roll had sounded over Newbern, and the Home Guard were actually called out. It seems that a force of rebels, under the supposition that our garrison was essentially weakened by the reconnoisance, came down to feel of our strength, but wisely concluded not to come too near, although succeeding in killing two of our picket guard, belonging to the Massachusetts 24th. I should have mentioned in my previous letter that a member of this regiment was shot at Chopper's Creek the same night we lost two men from the 44th. By the way, we have just received from a Richmond paper an account of this skirmish, by which we learn for the first time that one of our cavalry companies was annihilated, and that our general loss was very severe, while the rebels lost but two men killed and a few wounded. Per contra, veracious contrabands at Williamston told us of wagon-loads of rebel slain and wounded carried through that place. We thought Belger's battery was doing the business for them, and were quite prepared for the report given by the negroes.

The Newbern Progress, which is published under the supervision of the military authorities here, gives the following account of our expedition:

"FEDERAL RECONNOISANCE TO HAMILTON.—On the 3d inst., Major-General Foster, with about five thousand men, made a reconnoisance in force from Washington, N. C., towards Weldon, with the intention of taking Williamston and Hamilton, which points were strongly fortified by intrenchments, and also to interrupt the reported construction of iron-clads on the Roanoke River. The expedition advanced overland for some distance without meeting an enemy. The rebels, about three thousand strong, made a stand, however, at a place called Little Creek, but were repulsed with slight loss.

"Our troops pushed on to Williamston and Hamilton, where they executed a flank movement, with a fair prospect of bagging the whole rebel force, who, however, saved themselves by a hasty flight. The rebel fortifications about these places, which were more than three miles in length, and of a very formidable character, were destroyed by our troops. No iron-clads were found. The places taken were not garrisoned by General Foster, inasmuch as the rebels can be whipped out of them again at any time."

Last evening we were delighted to welcome the Massachusetts 45th and other regiments, by the Merrimac, Mississippi and Saxon. We regaled them with coffee, and listened with astonishment to their narrations of snow and sleighing in Boston last Sunday. The letters and papers they brought us, and which came by mail and one subsequent arrival, were inexpressibly welcome, and were devoured with even more avidity than our rations at the close of a day's march.

To-day the 44th underwent its first inspection by General Foster. Of course we put our best foot forward. Leather and brass and steel shone as they had not shone before since they left Readville. Spotless white handkerchiefs and gloves in the hands of the General's aids sought for soiling matter about our rifles, but generally without success. The General was pleased to compliment us. He was accompanied by a little daughter, who rode a pretty pony with childish grace.

Newbern has become quite a jolly place to live in. It is filled with Yankee jimcracks, ranging all the way from top-boots to preserved strawberries. The market supplies splendid Northern apples, Southern ditto, cider, honey, ginger cakes, crackers, fish, preserved meats and fruits, oysters, pickles, condensed milk, chocolate, sugar, tea, coffee, military goods, &c.   It is wonderfully convenient to be so near all these little comforts, *especially to those having a shot in the locker.*

Gingerbread, pies, and even apple-dumplings, are brought to us by the negroes in profusion, while the sutlers furnish us with butter, cheese, sardines, and all the main essentials of luxurious living.   Our regular rations are not to be sneezed at, although at present a scarcity of hops has thrown us back upon hard tack.   We are treated to beef steaks, excellent rice soups, fish, hash, &c.

The general health of the regiment continues good, although a few in each company are weakened by diarrhœa, and some few are yet suffering from colds and coughs contracted by our late exposures.   The majority of the men, however, were never in better condition.

It is, perhaps, needless for me to inform you that the published report of the capture of a large rebel force near Plymouth, was a canard.   I learn that the enterprising perpetrator of the story is under arrest.

----

NEWBERN, N. C., Nov. 19, 1862.

Newspaper correspondents are not allowed to give all the news in this department, and any apparent deficiencies in my letters in the way of military intelligence can thus be easily accounted for.   The Newbern Progress, I observe, omits to record the arrival of regiments, which would seem to be a very useless precaution, considering that the Boston and New York papers herald in advance the departure of every regiment for this department.   I also notice that they are industriously posting up the rebels concerning a prospective expedition to Texas. A government that can afford to divulge its military plans in this way must be strong indeed.

We have received a copy of the New York Herald of the 15th inst., giving a brief account of our skirmish near Williamston.   It is observed studiously to avoid giving the slightest credit to the 44th, which bore its full share of the brunt of the whole expedition, and acquitted itself in a manner to elicit the warm commendation of the General Commanding.

In my hurried account of our late march many incidents of the expedition were unavoidably omitted.   All secesh men who might be useful to the enemy, resident along the road, were taken prisoners.   Miserable looking fellows were they, as a rule, but quite handsome enough for their wives. In the house of one poor miserable paralytic wretch we found a double-barrelled gun, loaded and capped. "This is what picks off our men of nights." said a sergeant of cavalry, as he took possession of the shooter: and then, by a close examination, satisfied himself that the sick rebel was not playing possum. The scared and forlorn expression on the yellow and haggard face of his wife was a study for an artist.

As one decent looking farmer was taken from his house, an affectionate daughter followed the soldiers and besought them in shrieks of anguish to let her papa come back. Repeated assurances that her papa should not be hurt, seemed to afford her only very slight consolation.

Among our prisoners was a little curly-headed rebel sergeant who was taken captive at Roanoke Island and paroled. The contrabands in our train gave him the name of being a dreadfully severe master. He refused to take the oath, although once offering to do so at a time when he might have afforded his rebel friends valuable information of our strength and whereabouts. He managed his conversation with great shrewdness, and when, upon our return past his residence, he left us to go home, he no doubt chuckled over the information which he had artfully drawn from some of the garrulous fellows placed on guard over him.

Private Lane, detailed as wagoner from Co. D, and who upon our march did yeoman's service as forager, claims the "first blood." He was searching a rebel's house for fire-arms, and being forcibly resisted in his efforts to secure one of these weapons, used the butt of a fowling piece over the head of secesh with such good effect that all resistance ceased.

The morning after our affair with the rebels at Chopper's Creek, or Rawles' Mill, as the place is variously called, a party of us went to a neighboring house to fill our canteens at the well. Three good looking women, a grey-haired mother and two daughters, sat in the piazza. The younger ones were handsome, and one was a widow in weeds. The man of the house, a paralytic old gentleman, weighing three hundred and fifty pounds, sat in the centre of the hall running through the house. In the course of the artillery fire, the preceding night, a shot had passed through the floor of the piazza while the family were occupying it. The poor old man was too frightened to speak except in monosyllables. His wife besought us with streaming eyes to leave them alone—"they were only two poor old critters," although their son *had* been shooting at us from the woods a few hours before.  The young woman in weeds, pale and pensive, said little.  Her sister, who wouldn't acknowledge that she was frightened by the bombardment, boldly declared that she was a "seceder," and that "the meanest of all the critters was them as wouldn't stick up for their country."  One of our soldiers courteously suggested that we were sticking up for the *whole* country, while she was only sticking up for a fraction of it.  She replied that she was in favor of an undivided country so long as we could get along harmoniously, but when that became impossible, she became a "seceder."  "We believe as our men say," she added, as a clincher.

At Williamston, in one of the deserted mansions, some of our boys fell upon an old piano, which, during our first few hours' tarry at that place, although mingling its notes with the voices of sacrificed pigs, resounded vigorously with old familiar airs, speaking eloquently of home and friends.  The relic fever raged wildly at Williamston, and books, MSS., and trinkets, some of considerable rarity and value, were carried away by our soldiers.  The office of Judge Biggs, an ex-U. S. Senator, contributed largely to allay the craving for spoils and relics which unfortunately possesses too many of our men.

The last noticeable incident of the expedition was the arrest of the captain of the principal transport conveying our regiment.  In coming down the Roanoke River with a schooner in tow, crowded with troops, the schooner was so unaccountably run ashore that the captain of the steamer was superseded by the mate and confined in his own cabin.  After that we proceeded without much hindrance.  The summary manner in which military authorities avail themselves of transports is doubtless not a little aggravating to the sovereigns of the quarter-deck, unaccustomed as they are to rivals near the throne.

As we read now-a-days of our poor fellows upon the Potomac shivering o' nights, for the want of overcoats and proper shelter, we sympathize with them most deeply, as our late experience has enabled us to do.  It is difficult to exaggerate the discomfort of stretching one's self for sleep, without fire, upon wet ground, and that with wet, cold feet, growing colder and colder towards morning.  On one occasion we were driven to our feet by rain, and on another by intense cold.  We wonder that we endure these exposures, and not only live, but almost flourish under them.  Our experience has already taught us something of the wonderful endurance and elasticity of the human frame, which rusts out through the enervation of idleness and vicious habits faster than it wears out by the sturdy hardships of the soldier.

We are again settling into barrack life and drill.   Here is the daily order of performances :

Reveille, 6.30 A. M.; breakfast, 7; sergeant's report to adjutant, 7.15; surgeon's call, 7.30; guard mounting, 8; squad drills under sergeants, superintended by commissioned officers, 8.30 to 10; block drill for commissioned officers under lieut.-colonel, 10 to 11; company drill under lieutenants, 11 to 12; block drill for sergeants under captains, 11 to 12; dinner at 12; first sergeant's call, 1 P. M.; company drill, 1.30 to 2.30; battalion drill, 3 to 4; company parade, 4.30 : dress parade, 5; supper, 6; tattoo, 7.30; taps, 8.30.

Among other items of regimental news is the commissioning of Charles C. Soule, formerly adjutant of the Fourth Battalion, as second lieutenant of the Newton company, Captain Griswold, in place of Lieutenant Kendrick, promoted to the place made vacant by the resignation of First Lieutenant Forbes.   Lieutenant Soule had command of our camp in the absence of our regiment upon the expedition beyond Hamilton.   He is now in Boston upon recruiting service, and any of our friends who may desire to make him the guardian of Thanksgiving or Christmas packages on their way hither, will take notice.   We are already making arrangements for a Thanksgiving dinner as nearly like that New England institution as practicable.

We have named our camp " Stevenson," as a mark of esteem for the Colonel commanding our brigade.   At the christening, three hearty cheers were given for him.

NOVEMBER 20, 1862.

It rains easily here in November, and to-day the windows of heaven are opened wide.   We that should otherwise have been on drill, like it.   The poor fellows on guard do not.   The amount of letter-writing in this regiment is something astounding.   Each mail carries from the 44th scarcely less than fifteen hundred missives to friends in Massachusetts.   Pens and pencils are busy to-day.   Some are darning their stockings, and have reason to bless the foresight which prepared those little bags of yarn, needles, &c., which they received at the hands of Mrs. Otis.

---

NEWBERN, N. C., DEC. 1, 1862.

Thanksgiving Day, the 27th ult., was duly celebrated by the Massachusetts troops at this post.   It would not have been observed with more feeling and *eclat* by the same individuals at home.   It is to be questioned, even, if the viands of a New England Thanksgiving, smoking upon the home table, would have been eaten with so ardent a relish as that with which our somewhat ruder dainties were devoured in barracks. My observations were, of course, chiefly confined to our own regiment. Company F, as in most other things, took the lead, and dined together as a company. Their barracks and table presented a marvel of neatness and taste. The rough walls were half obscured with holly branches and flags. The long table was covered with a white cloth, crockery ware, and glass. Poultry, vegetables, sauces, pies, puddings, cakes, roast beef, oysters, coffee and dessert helped to make up their bill of fare : it was not found necessary to send beyond Newbern for luxuries contrasting so pleasantly with " hard tack and salt horse." The dinner was gotten up by the rank and file, and private Hopkinson presided. A series of " regular toasts " were offered, and the speeches which followed would have put to the blush the majority of after-dinner efforts in " our Athens." The President of the United States and the Old Commonwealth were fittingly eulogized, and the dear ones at home were pathetically alluded to in song and speech. In the evening Apollo and Terpsichore ruled the hour.

In most of the other barracks the companies dined luxuriously. In a few the company spirit proved insufficient to secure so much unanimity ; but there were numerous cheerful messes, ample spreads, and afterwards a due amount of colic. Companies G, E, H, C, D and A. and perhaps others, got up evening dances or literary entertainments. The day was made a complete holiday, all drill, and even dress parade, being omitted. The Massachusetts 5th, and some other regiments and companies, indulged in mock dress parades, which produced very side-splitting effects indeed. The acting Major of the Fifth appeared in a complete undress uniform of red flannel, most of the men with their garments inside out, and wearing haversacks upon their heads. There were several fine personations of Falstaff, and one man in armor, to wit, an army stove, through the door of which he made his observations. The manual presented some amusing varieties of the Hardee, and the first sergeants were ordered " to their posts—quick !" Altogether the Fifth are said to have equalled the best exhibition of the Antiques and Horribles. Among the spectators was Governor Stanley.

So passed Thanksgiving in the country of the enemy. We could not have asked for a jollier one, but God grant that the next may be in New England, and for new and more powerful reasons than has yet impelled us to perpetuate the example of the Pilgrims.

At dress parade Friday evening, Colonel Lee complimented the regiment for its appropriate observance of the previous day, and for the good order before and after taps.

As respects future military movements in the department, your correspondent is mum. We have but a few sick, and the few wounded are doing well.

We have organized a regimental choir under Charley Ewer, of Company D. Drum-Major Babcock has got his corps in good working order, and is now laboring industriously in organizing a band. We have the loan of a set of instruments, but they may be called for at an early day; so our friends in Boston may now gratify themselves in their long-cherished scheme of presenting us a set of instruments.

The Massachusetts 8th, Colonel Coffin, and the 51st, Colonel Sprague, arrived at Newbern last evening. We had the happiness of treating them to hot coffee.

I need scarcely remind the friends at home how anxiously we shall look for " boxes " between this and Christmas. The latest arrived transports were supposed to bring a great number of those interesting articles, and to-night a numerous squad was despatched to the town to bring them to camp. There proved to be about one box to each two hundred men. I will just mention that we have not seen the paymaster.

This letter and many others will be taken to Boston by Rev. Charles F. Barnard, whose familiar form appeared to us this evening at dress parade. He officiated at the evening services, and made some stirring remarks to the regiment. Mr. Barnard has one son in the 44th, and another in the 24th.

---

NEWBERN, N. C., DEC. 22, 1862.

A correspondent who marches with rifle and knapsack will not be expected to compete with the cavaliers of the New York press, whose business it is to glean facts and send them forward by the earliest and swiftest messengers. You will have heard that we have been on another expedition, the prominent results of which were three successful engagements with the enemy, and the destruction of a large railroad bridge on the road connecting Goldsboro' with Warrington. We marched one hundred and fifty miles in ten days, and came back to Newbern in a more dilapidated condition than after our trip to the vicinity of Tarboro'. The expedition included four brigades under General Wessell, lately stationed near Suffolk, Virginia, Colonel Stevenson, Colonel Amory, and Colonel Lee, of the 27th. The regiments were the Massachusetts 3d, 5th, 17th, 23d, 24th, 25th, 43d, 44th, 45th, 46th, and 51st; the New York 85th, 92d, and 96th; the Pennsylvania 85th, 101st, and 103d; New Jersey 9th; Connecticut 10th, and Rhode Island 5th. Besides these was a considerable force of cavalry and nearly fifty pieces of artillery, including Belger's Rhode Island and the New York 3d artillery. Altogether our force could not have fallen much below fifteen thousand men.

Our first two days' march up the Trent road was not marred by any extraordinary adventures. We were in heavy marching order, and experienced terrible fatigue. Straggling commenced the first day, and was kept up until our return. On the second day our progress was slightly impeded by trees felled across the road, the burning of a bridge, and a skirmish with the enemy's pickets, in which we killed some and took some prisoners. We saw one dead rebel stretched upon a piazza as we passed a house on our right, and marvelled at the stolid indifference of two or three white women who sat near the corpse and gazed at us as though nothing unusual had happened. At one point the column was confronted by a spunky secesh female, who, with a heavy wooden rake, stood guard over her winter's store of sweet potatoes. Her eye flashed defiance, but so long as she stood upon the defensive no molestation was offered her. When, however, she concluded to change her tactics, and slapped a cavalry officer in the face, gone were her sweet potatoes and other stores in the twinkling of an eye.

On Sunday, our fourth day from Newbern, we were drawn up in line of battle about one mile from Kinston, a large rebel town on the Neuse. The duty of the right wing of the 44th was to deploy as skirmishers and pass through a swamp to the right of the road, which was defended by a strong rebel battery near the river. We were *led* forward by Colonel Lee. As we approached the swamp, we met the wounded of the Massachusetts 45th and Connecticut 10th, who had preceded us. It was not a very reassuring spectacle, and we plunged knee deep into the mud and peat before us, under the firm expectation that bloody work awaited us as well as our predecessors. In this, however, we were happily disappointed. We found the swamp strewed with blankets and soldiers' gearing, and just upon the further outskirts of the place lay a number of the dead of the 45th. As we emerged into the opening beyond we expected to confront a force of rebel infantry, but were again agreeably disappointed. The first rebels we saw was a long file of rebel prisoners which were just then passing by us on our left. Advancing a few rods further to join our left wing, which had gone forward by the road, we had scarcely got in sight of our artillery before another squad of rebel soldiers issued from the wood between our guns and the river, with a flag of truce and delivered themselves up.

We soon knew by the cheers that went up that the day was ours. How it was achieved we did not exactly know then, but we heard of brave and gallant deeds by the Connecticut 10th, the New Jersey 9th and the Peninsula soldiers. You will have seen by the lists of killed and wounded that there was hard fighting, and that the rebels made a determined stand. After the smoke of battle had cleared away, we found ourselves in possession of a rebel battery and about five hundred prisoners. We found that we had possession of the bridge crossing the river to Kinston, the rebels having been forced to beat such a hasty retreat as not to have time to fire the structure. One man in attempting the operation by the aid of spirits of turpentine, burned himself to death. The rebels left loaded guns near the fire which they kindled, and one of them put an end to the life of Col. Gray of the New York 96th, who was assisting his men to extinguish the flames.

The scene of the conflict was the most beautiful which we have yet witnessed in North Carolina. It was an elevated field on the southerly shore of the Neuse, whose course is here marked by a fringe of fine trees through which the white buildings and spires of Kinston were observable a mile distant. The mangled condition of the trees and shrubbery near the road, or wherever the artillery or infantry guns ranged, gave proof of extremely hot work. Major Chambers, who commanded the 23d, said ten thousand rebel bullets whistled over the head of his regiment while it supported one of our batteries.

It is said that the enemy had a force of seven regiments under the command of Gen. Evans, of South Carolina. The men we took as prisoners were of the rawest and most miserable description. Some of them had been hurried down from Raleigh that morning. They regarded their captivity with great equanimity, not to say cheerfulness. They were doubtless all paroled. Among them were several field and line officers.

Sunday night we passed in Kinston, bivouacing on the borders of the town. As we passed through the streets upon our first entrance we found many bales of cotton piled up and set on fire. The Kinston rebels no doubt thought we were dying to get possession of their precious staple. Near the depot a great pile of corn was also on fire, and afforded a splendid bivouac blaze for some of our troops. A few Union people we found here. One lady hospitably entertained some of the officers, and afforded interesting information of the enemy's hopes and discomfiture. They confidently expected to hold the place, but left with great precipitancy, strewing the way with clothing, equipments, guns, &c.

The next day (Monday) we recrossed the river and proceeded towards Goldsboro'. Tuesday noon we reached Whitehall bridge, which, however, had been burned by the rebels, who were there in force to dispute our passage. As usual they were all under cover, with riflemen securely posted near the opposite bank. The ball opened with the thunder of artillery on both sides. At the same time several brigades of our infantry were hurried forward and deployed on either side the road to reply to the volleys of the sharpshooters in ambuscade. Our regiment was posted on the edge of a hill near the river, directly behind a Virginia rail-fence. Here we lay down and loaded and fired across the river, until we began to find ourselves the objects of particular attention. Eight of our men were killed or mortally wounded, and fourteen others less seriously injured. Of the killed, two men in Co. A were struck down by a solid shot, while we were hurrying forward to the post assigned us.

Our place soon became so warm that Belger's battery of artillery was sent to our relief, when we fell back and supported it while it shelled the opposite shore. But the sharpshooters were too securely posted to be disturbed, and commenced picking off our horses, greatly to the disgust of Capt. Belger, who soon ascertained that he was throwing his shot away. In the meantime the rebel artillery had been silenced, and the column soon resumed its march up the southerly side of the river. During the engagement at Whitehall, a company of sharpshooters was hastily organized, and it is believed that some of the rebels got a Roland for their Oliver. "Old Stars," of Co. D, who is equally familiar with shooting stars and shooting sticks, is confident of bringing down a man. Col. Lee and Major Dabney,.both experienced riflemen, took part with the sharpshooters, and were also noticed to present somewhat too conspicuous marks for the riflemen on the other side. The daring of all our field officers and chaplain has been established beyond question. None of the rest of the regiment have been so much exposed as they.

Beside destroying the bridge at Whitehall, the rebels destroyed two gunboats constructing at that point, and thereby saved us the trouble of the operation.

The following is a complete list of the killed and wounded at the battle of Whitehall :

Co. A. Killed—Albert L. Butler, D. Tyler Newcomb, J. Mason Slocumb, M. R. Meagher. Wounded—A. H. Everett, A. S. May, J. F. Berry, Sergt. J. F. Clark, A. K. Tappan, J. W. Greenwood, Wm. Bamford.

Co. B. Wounded (accidental)—A. H. Everett.

Co. C. Killed—Sergt. A. Stacy Courtis, Corp. E. H. Curtis, Antonio F. Pollo.

Co. K. Killed—Geo. E. Noyes.

Co. D. Wounded—Charles C. Ewer, Frederic Jackson.

Co. F. Wounded—J. F. Dean.

Co. G. Wounded—Francis E. Lincoln, E. S. Fisher.

Co. H. Wounded—Sergt. Howe, E. C. Crosby.

George H. Colby, of Company D, detailed for duty on the signal corps, was seriously wounded in one of his arms while going up the river Neuse, with his party, to act in concert with the expedition. Their boat was fired at a number of times, and several rebel batteries were subsequently cleaned out by our gunboats, which now go up within a short distance of Kinston, where they met our returning column with a supply of provisions.

A few miles beyond Whitehall we bivouaced for the night, and the next day pressed on to Everettsville, a short distance from Golbsboro', where we had the happiness of destroying a long tressel-work bridge on the railroad connecting Goldsborough with Wilmington. Here again we met the enemy in force, but as our regiment was held in reserve, I have only a hearsay statement of the incidents of the fight. The cannonading was long and fierce, and the rebels made a dash to capture one of our batteries, but were repulsed with very serious slaughter. I hear they attempted the flag of truce dodge once too often. Whether or not it was the intention of General Foster to push on to Goldsborough, it became apparent at this point that we could safely advance no farther, owing to the scarcity of our provisions and artillery ammunition, so we turned about and went back to Newbern, where our advance arrived last Saturday night.

The expedition was favored with extraordinarily fine weather; but even under this most favorable circumstance, the march was one of unusual severity. Some of the Peninsular soldiers said it outdid their previous experience, and that they never before witnessed so much straggling. We bivouaced every night without shelter, but were kept tolerably comfortable by our rubber and woollen blankets.

The assembled bivouac fires of fifteen thousand men present a spectacle of rare beauty. I notice that a recent number of Leslie's Illustrated contains a graphic and truthful picture of "Going into Camp." The rail gathering is to the life. You can imagine how much we are indebted to the rail fences of Secessia. They give us comfortable fires, hot coffee, and sometimes shelter itself. I can hardly conceive how we could live without them. Perhaps we are equally indebted to the pigs and potatoes of the country, for soldiers certainly never could march ten days upon hard tack and coffee alone. Upon leaving the barracks each man is provided with a little bag of coffee and sugar mixed; so he always has at hand the means for a comforting and strengthening draught. This is found extremely convenient in the many cases where the cooks and wagons fail to come to time by reason of break-downs or other delays on the road.

I have spoken of stragglers upon the march. There are two or three distinct kinds of straggling. One is involuntary—the result of sickness or exhaustion. Another comes from laziness or the want of a spirited determination to bear up; and another from cowardice. Do not imagine that because a man enlists and goes to the wars that he necessarily does his whole duty as a soldier. There are no better opportunities for shirking than those afforded the soldier. It was noticeable upon our late march that whenever cannonading commenced at the head of the column, as it did day after day, scores of men commenced falling out and laying down by the side of the road. This was peculiarly the case with some of the old regiments, and I think there were few of the new ones but exhibited their cowards and sneaks on these occasions in this way.

I am now obliged to close this hurried and meagre account, asking the reader to remember that among the really "played out" soldiers of the late expedition is "Corporal."

P. S. I am authorized to thank numerous friends for many Christmas boxes. God bless the thoughtful friends at home.

---

NEWBERN, N. C., JAN. 2, 1863.

The proprietor of the Herald has the warm thanks of the 44th regiment for a kind remembrance in the shape of a generous bundle of Sunday Heralds, evidently made up without regard to the increased price of paper. I believe it is the pretty general opinion of our boys

that no paper quite so well meets the requirements of Massachusetts
soldiers as the Sunday Herald,—a fact which our great constituency
of friends in Boston appears to appreciate.  Its department of military
news is the most complete given by any Boston paper; and the same
may be said of its musical and dramatic columns, to which our theatre-
loving and theatre-hungry boys turn with an ever sharpening appetite.
The spice and point of its editorial articles are not less admired.  So
much by way of encouragement to the hard-working fellows at No. 6
Williams Court.

Since our return from Goldsboro', a little more than a week ago, we
have been considerately respited from drill and work generally.  A ten
days' tension of our utmost physical power left us in a very "chawed-
up" condition, independent of the colds contracted and the feet made
sore; and we stood in good need of the week's rest which has been
granted us.  I am wondering if the troops in this department are an
exception to the general rule, and if newspaper correspondents really
tell the truth when they assert the anxiety of the soldiers of the
Potomac and elsewhere for advances, forward movements, &c. &c.
I have yet to be introduced to the soldier who desires a repetition of
these little excursions of Gen. Foster, and who wouldn't give his nine
months' pay and bounty for the certainty of serving his country as well
by remaining at Newbern during the rest of his term of service.  At
the same time, I do not know but that we are as brave and patriotic
as the average.  Let me assure you, dear friends at home, that none
beside the soldier can fully apprehend the full tests of patriotism, or
the difference between preaching and practice as applied to love of
country.

The soldier who unmurmuringly meets and performs his duties of
hardship and danger must be provided with something of that divine
armor which fits him to be a soldier of the cross.  The man who says
he loves to face the "leaden rain and iron hail" of battle is either a
liar or a monstrosity.  No man who cares for life and friends can go
into battle without a natural shudder and dread.  The wonder is that
duty and pride are strong enough in any man to urge him forward into
the very teeth of death.  Let us be charitable as possible toward the
white-livered wretches who fall out of the ranks at the first bidding
of the cannon's voice.

Among the severely wounded at Whitehall was Charley Ewer, the
regimental chorister.  The sweetness of his voice was the type of a
character which had endeared him greatly to his comrades.  He was

shot through one of the lungs, and his condition is most critical. The places he made musical are now dumb and sad. We hope a deeper gloom may not settle on them.

Our new band is making rather wonderful progress. They are a jolly set of fellows, the band, with no marching, no fighting, no drilling, no guarding to do. Hardly an even thing, perhaps: but, then, the band is a great ornament at inspections and dress parades, and we can't help feeeling some pride in it.

Since the holidays commenced the friends of the men in the regiment have overwhelmed us with the bounties and luxuries of home. Here are the contents of one box that came under the especial observation of your correspondent, and which he regards as a model in its way: tea, coffee, sugar, butter, pepper, salt, capsicum, cheese, gingerbread, confectioner's cakes, bologna sausage, condensed milk, smoked halibut, pepper-box, camp knife, matches, ink, mince pies, candy, tomato ketchup, apples, horse radish, emery paper, sardines, cigars, smoking tobacco, candles, soap, newspapers, pictorials, letters, pickles, and *cholera mixture*. The opening of this box, and the examination and display of its contents, furnished an evening of rare enjoyment. The arrival and distribution of these boxes at the Quartermaster's are attended by some very animated scenes. I am sorry to say that Mr. Sutler Grant's schooner is detained in the stream by red tape. He has a number of boxes for us.

Christmas was less extensively observed than Thanksgiving at Newbern, although not a few of us were enabled to indulge in a dinner a little better than usual. One or two of the barracks were trimmed with evergreen, and something like amusement was attempted by the aid of contraband minstrelsy and dancers.

Last night, New Year's, we were favored with the

SECOND

# DRAMATIC AND MUSICAL ENTERTAINMENT

BY THE

## 44TH REGIMENTAL DRAMATIC ASSOCIATION.

| | |
|---|---|
| Prologue (original) . . | Henry T. Reed. |
| Overture . | . Band. |
| Recitation (selected) | F. D. Wheeler. |
| Song . . . . | . Quartette Club. |
| Recitation . | C. A. Chase. |
| Recitation (humorous) . . | . E. L. Hill. |

BAND.

After which the Grand Trial Scene from

## THE MERCHANT OF VENICE.

| | |
|---|---|
| Shylock | H. T. Reed. |
| Duke | W. Howard. |
| Antonio | D. F. Safford. |
| Bassanio | F. D. Wheeler. |
| Gratiano | J. H. Waterman. |
| Portia | L. Miller. |
| Solanio | F. A. Sayers. |

### BAND.

Followed by

## A GRAND MINSTREL SCENE.

| | |
|---|---|
| Opening Chorus | Company. |
| Louisiana Lowlands | H. Howard. |
| Dolly Day | F. A. Sayers. |
| Shells of the Ocean | H. Howard. |
| Susianna Simpkins | F. A. Sayers. |
| Ham Fat Man | J. H. Myers. |

Concluding with

## A TERRIBLE CAT-ASS-TROPHE ON THE NORTH ATLANTIC RAILROAD.

Characters by the Company.

| | |
|---|---|
| Director | H. T. Reed. |
| Assistant Manager | D. F. Safford. |
| Secretary | W. Howard. |
| Treasurer | J. M. Waterman. |

Executive Committee: F. D. Wheeler, L. Miller, F. A. Sayers.

The order of exercises was upon neatly-printed handbills.

Since the Federal occupation of Kinston, work upon the railroad from Newbern to the former town has been vigorously prosecuted: but recently the rebels have taken a characteristic fancy to drive in our workmen and rip up their work.

The troops in North Carolina have been constituted an army corps, of which several divisions are to be formed in due time. Brigadier-General Wessells has already been assigned to command a division. Col. Stevenson has received his stars, and his brigade will be the second of Wessells's division, the first being composed of the Pennsylvania and New York troops, lately under his command as brigadier, and now under Gen. Hunt, from the Potomac army. The other divisions will probably be commanded by some of the new Brigadiers in this department, of whom one is Gen. Hickman, lately Colonel of the New Jersey 9th. Gen. Stevenson's brigade comprises the Mass.

8th, 24th, and 44th, the Rhode Island 5th, and the Conn. 10th. The 44th will be the only new regiment in Gen. Wessells's division.

We are glad our friends at the North derive so much satisfaction and encouragement from our late raid up the valley of the Neuse. Since our return, it has formed a subject of lively contemplation among those engaged in it. I notice by the rebel papers that secesh was well apprised of two facts about us, to wit: that we were short of artillery ammunition, and also of provisions. It occurred to your correspondent that the cannoniers were quite too communicative of the first fact. The blabbing of soldiers is really one of the greatest of nuisances, not to say curses, connected with our army. Supposed facts and conjectures are retailed by them with never slacking industry, and with equal assurance and recklessness, a hear-say or rumor immediately taking rank with truth itself in the minds and mouths of a miserable set of *quid nuncs* which infest every company of every regiment.

As to our being out of provisions, our systematic amd extensive foraging was the best proof of the low condition of our hard tack and salt horse. There were days when we got very hungry indeed, when visions of past luxuries haunted the mind like torturing ghosts. Baked beans chiefly afflicted the soul of your correspondent. They would not down at his bidding. Neither would that little coffee-pot on the warm range at midnight, where it was wont to stand when I came home from the labor of the newspaper sanctum. We found way-side turnip patches sources of great relief and substantial refreshment, but our chief subsistence was the pigs, cattle, and sweet potatoes of the country. With a little lard, a little corn meal, and sweet potatoes sliced and fried, we were soon enabled to forget a day's fatigue. Poultry and slices of tenderloin sometimes fell to the lot of a few who supped royally.

During the fight at Everettsville the soldiers of the reserve busied themselves with eating turnips and gazing at the conflict. In the midst of the cannonade, a lively charge was made by our brigade on a mound of sweet potatoes between us and the enemy. Subsequently, at night, while we deployed in the woods in anticipation of a pursuit of our retiring column, we consoled ourselves by munching the sweet potatoes we had stowed in our pockets and haversacks.

That night's countermarching is never to be forgotten for its wild and picturesque beauty. Fires were running on either side of the road. The ground was spread with a carpet of flame, and the resinous pine were as pillars of fire. The beautiful scenes thus afforded cheered our march wonderfully, and engraved pictures on the mind which will endure as long as memory.

Among other items of regimental news I will mention the resignation of Captain Reynolds, on account of ill health. Captain Lombard is much reduced by illness, and will probably resign,— in which event the regiment will lose one of its best and bravest officers. Capt. Lombard and his first lieutenant Geo. Lombard both distinguished themselves for pluck and coolness at the midnight skirmish near Williamston.

------

NEWBERN, N. C., JAN. 18, 1863.

The uncertainty of the mails to and from this place, and the unaccountable delay in the publication of some of my letters, are the causes which have operated to prevent my writing with the frequency of a few weeks ago. If I could say it without appearance of egotism, I should like to observe that few correspondents beside "Corporal" can have stronger incentives to continue his communications, if he might judge by the reception which the friends of the 44th have given his letters thus far, and the acknowledgements which it has been his pleasure to receive. So much in return.

My stock of regimental gossip is not abundant this time. Since my last we have been visited by the paymaster. How it happens that nine months' regiments, and bounty regiments at that, are paid off, while old regiments, which have not seen the paymaster for six or nine months, are skipped, passeth the understanding of even the favored ones like ourselves. It is a circumstance certainly not calculated to improve the relations between the old and new regiments, none the best at present.

Since the advent of the paymaster, we have had a less agreeable camp visitor in the shape of malarious fever. Several deaths from this complaint have already occurred, and a number of dangerous cases are in the hospital. The malady attacks with great suddenness, and is attended with much delirium and distress. As a measure of prevention the regiment is served with quinine every evening.

Many of the regiments are renewedly cheered and made grateful by the reception of home comforts. Your correspondent must be pardoned for laying some stress on this pleasant feature of our experience. The delayed schooners of Sutler Grant have at last arrived with their precious freights. Time, it is to be confessed, had made its mark upon some of the poultry and pastry, but that which had been sealed in tin cans or boxes arrived in fine condition, although nearly a month in transitu. As friends express themselves in much doubt as to what is best to send, here are the contents of a box recently received, which may be taken as a model: A large sealed tin box of mince pies and cake; a large sealed tin box of cake; a large paper box of ditto; a tin box of sugar; a tin box of pepper; a jar of pickles; a box of eggs; together with apples, pears, pins, stationery, and last but not least, letters. A portion of one of the latter articles I subjoin. It may also be regarded as a model:

"There are so many articles we wish to send you, but so few which we feel sure will reach you unspoiled, that it has required considerable thought and discussion on our part, in regard to the particular articles which shall be sent. But if you take one half the pleasure in receiving and consuming them that it has given us to prepare them, we shall be more than happy.

. "I hope the vessel which carries out this little box may go freighted with many good things prepared by loving hearts and willing hands to give comfort to the soldiers.

"The most that I can do for you and the brave men who have so cheerfully and nobly gone forth to put down this wicked rebellion, seems so little, when compared with the sacrifices you have made, that it seems hardly worth thinking of; and yet, when we send off our loved ones to this terrible war, we feel the sacrifices are not *all* on your side.

"I have a dear young brother in Banks's Expedition, who has gone to lay down his young life, if needed; and hard as it was to give him up, I feel more proud of him than I ever did before.     *     *

"Another thing we have to wonder about, and that is, whether you may not be in want of some stockings. Those long wearisome marches you have made must wear out shoes and stockings as well as feet.     * 
*     *     Now, be it known unto you, it is *no* trouble to do what we can for the soldier, particularly when that soldier is a friend. It would give us untold pleasure to supply you with some of those very useful articles, if you will let your wants be known."

"Corporal" and other innocent persons have lately experienced the novel sensation of a night drill, as an atonement for the sins of a few young gentlemen addicted to throwing hard bread about the barracks, and charging pipes and candles with gunpowder. This species of vicarious punishment, in which officers and privates are alike involved, is one of the odd peculiarities of military justice to which we sometimes have to submit with the best grace possible under the circumstances.

The favor of our friends at home is bespoken in behalf of a memorial volume of the 44th Regiment soon to be put in press under the editorship of Mr. Safford, of Company F. Its contents will be furnished by the members of the regiment, and will have exclusive reference to its history.

Whatever it may lack in completeness and finish will be easily attributable to the circumstances attending the compilation of the work, the editor and contributors being working soldiers.

We are in the occasional receipt from Boston of third-hand private reports reflecting upon the bravery of our regiment upon various occasions; and now, coupled with one of these slanders, comes a story charging Quartermaster Bush with gross and contemptible frauds upon the men, such as stealing their boxes, blankets and other articles sent by friends at the North. The last story, absurd as it is, is as true as the first, and both, I hardly need say, are malicious falsehoods—the one class of reports being systematically manufactured and circulated by men in one or two of the old regiments from Massachusetts, who will never forgive us because we were voted bounties *after* we had enlisted.

Since writing the above my attention has been called to a paragraph in a letter "from the 27th and 46th Regiments," in which the 44th Regiment is accused of refusing to charge at the battle of Kinston. The accusation is wholly and unqualifiedly false. The 44th did all it was told to do at Kinston, and it was personally complimented for its behavior by General Foster, as we marched by him into town. I confess that I undertake to reply to these slanders with very little patience. The individual who was induced to send them north for publication showed less sagacity than the reporter of the New York Herald, who was actually approached with a bribe to make certain statements derogatory to the 44th, and touching points of which he could have no personal knowledge. I have this from the Herald reporter's own mouth; and the reader will judge how far it goes to confirm the suspicion of a systematic purpose to do us an injury.

Lieutenant Weld has been elected Captain of Company K, in place of Captain Reynolds, resigned; and Second Lieutenant Brown, who becomes First Lieutenant, is succeeded by Sergeant Parkinson. Lieutenant George H. Lombard succeeds to the captaincy of Company C, by the resignation of Captain Jacob H. Lombard, and Sergeant Hedge becomes First Lieutenant. Lieutenant Briggs, of this company, is serving on the signal corps.

The names of those who have recently died in camp, of malarious fever, are Pollitz and Moody, of Company F; Kimball, of Company G; and Moulton, of Company C. The prevalence of this disease is attributed to the dryness of the season. It is not confined to one regiment. When the swamps which surround us are filled with rain, the cause will be removed.

At dress parade last evening the following order was read:

"In consideration of and as a reward for their brave deeds at Kinston, Whitehall and Goldsborough, the Commanding General directs that the regiments and batteries which accompanied the expedition to Goldsborough inscribe upon their banners these victories:

KINSTON, DECEMBER 14TH, 1862.

WHITEHALL, DECEMBER 16TH, 1862.

GOLDSBOROUGH, DECEMBER 17TH, 1862.

The Commanding General hopes that all future fields will be so fought that the record of them may be kept by inscription on the banners of the regiments engaged."

---

NEWBERN, N. C., JAN. 23, 1863.

The first grand Terpsichorean festival of the New Year in our regiment transpired on the evening of the 20th instant, in the barracks of Co. D. The much lamented absence of the feminine element was in part atoned for by female apparel donned for the occasion by a number of young men with smooth faces and an eye to artistic effect. If Jenkins had been present his pencil would have waxed eloquent over the superb attire and tasteful colors of the magnificent blonde, Miss C. D. N. His page would have glowed with lover-like panegyrics of the tall and peerless, white-robed queen of the night, Miss G. F. B. Good taste, however, might have suggested that the former was a little too *en bon point*, as well as too demonstrative in her personal decorations, and that the latter was a trifle tall for the breadth of her raiment. But when Jenkins came to the Misses C. F. W., J. H. W., W. G. R. and especially to Miss C. W. S., of East Boston, he would assuredly have "slopped over" in his characteristic manner. Not, however, because these Hebes were less faulty in toilet than the others, for a critical eye might have suggested dresses higher in the neck, longer in skirt, and less protuberant in the rear; less suggestive, in short, of those gay and festive occasions which have rendered Joe Clash and North street immortal the world over. Some of the gallants of the young women were scarcely less stunning in their make up. The insignia of military office, from that of Major Generals to Lieutenants, extensively prevailed. Dancing, of course, was the order of the night; a fiddler was engaged, and

> "When music arose with its voluptuous swell,
> Soft eyes looked love to eyes which spake again,
> And all went merry as a marriage bell."

The following is the

### ORDER OF DANCES.

1. SICILIAN CIRCLE, . . . . . . . . . . . . . . . March to Tarboro'.
2. QUADRILLE, . . . . . . . . . . . . . . . . . New England Guards.
3. POLKA QUADRILLE, . . . . , . . . . . . . . . . Kinston Gallop.
4. QUADRILLE, . . . . . . . . . . . . . . . . , . . . . Yankee Doodle.

#### INTERMISSION.

Waltz, Polka Redowa, Schottische.

5. QUADRILLE, . . . . . . . . . . . . . . . Bloody 44th Quickstep.
6. LES LANCIERS, . . . . . . . . . . . . . Connecticut 10th March.
7. QUADRILLE, . . . . . . . . . . . . . . . . . . . . . Lee's March.
8. CONTRA (*Virginia Reel*), . . . . . . . . . . Rebels' Last Skedaddle.

In this connection I will introduce the managerial card, which was as follows:

### GRAND BALL.

SIR:—The pleasure of your company, with ladies, is respectfully solicited at a Grand Ball, to be held in the Grand Parlor of the FIFTH AVENUE HOTEL, (No. 4 Newbern,) on TUESDAY EVENING, January 20th, 1863.

The Management beg leave to state that nothing will be left undone on their part to make it *the* party of the season.

#### MANAGERS.

C. H. DEMERITT,          W. HOWARD,          J. E. LEIGHTON.

#### COMMITTEE OF ARRANGEMENTS.

| Benj. F. Burchsted, | C. D. Newell, | W. G. Reed, | H. D. Stanwood, |
| W. E. Savery, | F. A. Sayer, | F. M. Flanders, | H. Howard, |
| J. B. Gardner, | Joe Simonds, | Charles Adams, | G. W. Hight. |

#### MUSIC.

Quintzelbottom's Grand Quadrille and Serenade Band,
(*One Violin.*)

TICKETS $00.03 EACH, TO BE HAD OF THE MANAGERS.

☞ *No Postage Stamps or Sutler's Checks taken in payment.*

N. B.  LADIES will be allowed to smoke.

Persons wishing carriages will please apply to LIEUT. WHITE, of the Ambulance Corpse.

Persons wishing anything stronger than Water are referred to the "Sanitary."

The managers were decorated with official rosettes, a solid square of hard tack forming the centre of each. Even some of the belles of the evening were resplendent with pendant jewels cut from the same tenacious mineral.

That nothing might be wanting to revive the memories of Clash's Hall, a bar was improvised inside the sliding door where we get our rations, and here the cooks busily regaled the dancers with water, and molasses and water, from a bottle and a single tumbler, while announcing, by means of placards over the window, "Splendid New Drinks," in the shape of quinine and diarrhœa mixture No. 3, names forever associated with and articulate in the surgeon's matutinal bugle-call. The bar soon began to show its effects in the shape of cocked hats, awry toilets, loud-mouthed controversies, and, at last, fighting. The intervention of an active but diminutive policemen was invoked. He was a little man, but chewed tobacco with a serious determination, which boded danger to evil doers. His services in keeping back the crowd and quelling disturbances in the vicinity of the bar were in constant requisition. Not unfrequently his badge was seen tossing in the midst of a riotous crowd, and he was reported to be once seen skedaddling before a slightly superior force. He was noticed as being very familiar with your reporter, whom he furnished with considerable doubtful information about his own operations.

At the proper hour refreshments were served. "A beautiful slave," in the person of Mr. West Williams, heretofore mentioned in these letters, entered with two trays containing severally hard tack and salt horse. His advent was hailed with the same shouts and swaying of the crowd as usually attend the administration of our rations. The tack and horse vanished, and the dance proceeded with various divertisements to the end.

We had many visitors, including Colonel Lee and staff, all of whom evinced their intense satisfaction with what they heard and saw.

It is expected that other balls, including a masquerade, will succeed this affair.

A soldier's life is one of curious contrasts. Although *not* always gay, it has the jolliest kind of episodes. It affords the two emotional extremes. One day finds him in the midst of hilarity and social enjoyment, the next in the blood and carnage of battle, with friends falling all about him

"Thick as autumnal leaves in Valambrosa."

But an hour or two before the festivities recounted above, a slow-moving procession with muffled drum and reversed arms, moved from our lines with the remains of a much-loved comrade suddenly stricken down with the malarious fever. His name was Boynton, of Company G. A day or two previously, Corporal Upham of the same company died of the same disease.

---

NEWBERN, N. C., JAN. 27, 1863.

The prevalence of malarious fever among some of the soldiers in this department at this season, has created a little excitement, and I hope no exaggerated stories concerning it will reach the ears of our friends at the North. Since my last but two fatal cases have occurred, making eight in all. The last two deceased were Bradbury of Co. C, and Ingraham of Co. F.

Malarious fever, although characteristic of this locality in summer, was not anticipated here after the early frosts; but the succeeding severe drouth so reduced the bulk of water in the neighboring swamps as to leave a margin of mud, which has sent forth the fever poison. It is not sure, however, that our miserably contracted barracks have nothing to do with this disease.

While by the army regulations of England and France, each soldier in barracks is allowed a thousand cubic feet of air and space, we are allowed but two hundred and fifty in which to live and move and have our being; in which to eat and sleep, and read and write, and to store our effects. English and French barracks, generous as they are in space, are still provided with a commissary room in which to store any private rations which the men may fortunately possess; but American soldiers must make bunk-fellows of their butter, pies and pickles, or go without them. Then again, our barracks at Newbern are constructed of wet, unseasoned lumber, fresh from unhealthy swamps, so that upon the walls and roof of some of them, green mould gathers. All these circumstances are at least suggestive of something; if they are not, what's the matter? There are certainly no reasons why American barracks should not be the largest and best in the world.

We are surely not deficient in space, materials, or in constructive ingenuity, among the soldiers who are detailed to build and fit up quarters. No sane man would herd cattle together so closely as we are herded, for fear of breeding distemper. They are well-settled facts that soldiers upon the march, and bivouacing every night in the open air, are in better health than when living in barracks; and that marching and bivouacing cure the colds contracted by means of frequent sudden changes from close barracks to the open air.

In my last I gave you some account of an extemporized ball in the barrack of Co. D. Since then a grand masquerade has been held under the auspices of Co. E, our nearest left hand neighbor. Only a few hours were given to preparation, but the affair assumed an extent, as well as an appearance of elegance and grotesque humor not a little surprising, considering the limited resources of soldiers in camp. The members of the regiment were forewarned of the entertainment by the following notice:

### BAL MASQUE.

A Grand Regimental *Bal Masque* will be held to-night, Jan. 24th, at the barrack of Co. E. None admitted except commissioned officers and those *en costume.*

The restriction was of little avail. Those who failed to pass the door keepers entered at the ventilators, and there was soon assembled the largest audience of the season. There were many masked and assumed characters, but the favorite and prevailing assumption was that of a girl. This was uniformly excellent, showing beyond doubt a close and enthusiastic devotion to the study of the character in the original. If you may trust the taste of *your* Jenkins, Miss K., of Co. F, was the belle of the occasion, although our public opinion is divided between that lady and Miss A., of Co. G, Miss R., of Co. E, the Misses H. and the Misses S., of Co. D, Miss H., of Co. A, and some others. I regret the poverty of vocabulary that prevents my describing their costumes. All of them were tasteful and some elegant. One lady of color attracted a large share of attention. Several personations of the Prince of Darkness were voted admirable. Not the worst Satan was a young divinity student of Co. D, who had evidently studied his *role.* Bird o' Freedom Sawin was there as a Pilgrim Father. There were harlequins, clowns, policemen, men of impenetrable visage, and one venerable monk with crucifix and beads. The barrack was brilliantly lighted by the aid of chandeliers, and there were, of course, music and dancing. Nearly all our officers were present, including the field and staff, together with several officers and privates from our excellent neighbor, the gallant Connecticut 10th, endeared to us alike by their signal bravery in the field of battle, and their cordial friendship toward us as a regiment.

We are adding to the defensive strength of Newbern. Rumor has it that the rebels are in strong force at Kinston. The situation of affairs in Virginia, and the growing importance of Gen. Foster's command, render the report more than probable. The feint of an attack, or the probability of it, has not prevented the embarkation from this place of a large expeditionary force for some point or points to us unknown, but doubtless of vital importance to the rebels. The result of its operations will reach you in good time. Unexpectedly to ourselves and to every one else, our regiment is left behind to help guard Newbern, now deemed by some the post of danger. The 45th is doing provost-guard duty in Newbern.

--------

FEBRUARY 1, 1863.

If Leigh Hunt, who discoursed so eloquently of the comforts of a bed, could have added to his genius the experience of a soldier, his bed panegyrics would have been moving indeed. The leisurely process of disrobing preparatory for the smooth comfort of clean sheets may not inaptly be compared to the change from the heavy, crawling chrysalis to the winged and airy insect radiant of a new experience. I forget whether or not Leigh Hunt made some such comparison as this; but he did dilate upon the positive luxury springing from the contact of two legs —to wit, your own two legs—after a day's cruel separation by the nether integuments which custom has rendered indispensable. If we survive our term of service, shall we not enjoy a bed? With limbs and trunks that have not pressed a sheet for nine months—limbs subjected to an intermitting friction of coarse flannel night and day for three-fourths of a year, in frigid bivouac and unyielding bunks—we certainly shall be prepared to experience and sing the pleasures of a bed when at last we come to the enjoyment of that luxury.

The Fry has arrived with our boxes. Besides the many containing good things to eat were several filled with not less useful offerings in the shape of stockings, wristers, sleeping caps, &c., made and contributed by some of our young friends of the gentler sex, who accompanied their gifts with anonymous notes, or notes bearing the signatures of "Betsey Baker" and other mythical young women. Contrary to newspaper rules the editor of this paper must allow me to take notice of these communications.

"Betsey Baker" writes:

"May these socks prove a safeguard against all bullets. If they prove such inform" &c., &c.

Thank you, dear, I will.

" Nelly Bly " writes :

" Would that I were with you to darn your socks for you ! If you want me to come, send " &c., &c.

" Mary of the Wild Moor " writes :

" Will the receiver of these socks please send me an account of the first march he takes with them ?"

This letter was commenced on board the transport steamer North-erner, an old lake boat, which is now transporting the 44th Regiment from Newbern to Plymouth, N. C. The Northerner is a spacious, comfortable old craft, and we are far better commoded on board of her than we were on the Merrimac, which conveyed us from Boston, or the George Collins, which afterwards carried us to Washington and then back to Newbern from Plymouth. Some of us really rejoice in the possession of staterooms, but the majority are contented to stretch themselves upon the floors of the spacious and well-lighted saloons, where at night we lie at every angle, and sleep like bricks. The stores by the Fry and other arrivals are serving us a good purpose while we are away from the comforts of the barracks. We haven't our daily soft bread, fresh meat and coffee twice a day, but our knapsacks are filled with preserved meats and fruits, apples, cakes, cheese, butter, &c., and the craving for food born of sea air is more than satisfied. Our regular rations of hard tack and salt meat at the bottom of our haversacks will keep until we need them.

We like these occasional aquatic trips. They are so good for the health and spirits of the men, that we half suspect our excellent surgeon had a voice in the planning of this last expedition. Newbern is hardly desirable as a place of long-continued residence, although an admirable and easily-defended military post. The band (our band) are with us, with their instruments. Their muskets are at Newbern, hence I conclude our expedition is not intended to be a very sanguinary one.

FEBRUARY 2, 1863.

We arrived at Plymouth about half past three this afternoon, and were glad to be informed that we were to retain our comfortable quarters on board the steamer until the next day. The cooks went on shore and made us coffee, and we supped comfortably. The evening opened beautifully, with a singularly bright moon, and the boys were in high spirits. Groups gathered upon the deck and sung glees. The saloon was cleared for a dance, and the light fantastic was tripped to the music of two fifes. The band took a position upon the hurricane deck, and discoursed their best strains. About the fires on the shore were groups of agile contrabands, delighting a number of spectators with their unique dances and songs. Altogether, a more cheering and picturesque scene could not well be imagined.

FEBRUARY 3, 1863.

We awoke this morning to find the ground white with snow, and the air thick with flakes, driven by a high wind. The scene was decidedly New Englandish, and contrasted curiously with that of the preceding evening. The climate of the " Sunny South " is certainly not without its freaks. We shall remain on board to-day, we are happy to be informed.

Plymouth shows sad marks of the recent rebel raid upon that town. Nearly fifty houses were burned by them, and the court-house, where our little force rallied, is thickly marked with their artillery shots. Upon our arrival the place was garrisoned by two companies of the Massachusetts 27th, one of the 3d, and a small force of North Carolina Cavalry. Three or four gunboats are also here, and it is rumored that we are to act in concert with them in an attack upon Rainbow Bluff, where a North Carolina regiment (the 17th, the same which we routed at Rawle's Mill, on the third of November,) is said to be strongly entrenched. Rainbow Bluff commands the Roanoke River, a very few miles this side of Hamilton, and over thirty miles from Plymouth. We find here a North Carolina deserter who sets the rebel loss at Kinston at five hundred. The rebel skedaddle from that place was of the most confused description. We are gratified to learn, as we do from the same source, that we did the rebels serious detriment at Whitehall, a fact which their hidden position would not permit us to know at the time. The enemy had an excellent view of us, and their riflemen were ordered to make General Stevenson, whom they recognized, a particular mark.

FEBRUARY 4, 1863.

We remained at Plymouth yesterday. The right wing of the regiment was transferred from the steamer to a large storehouse on the wharf. It was a cold day and we had no fires in the building, so the boys wandered over the town, and made themselves comfortable in negro cabins, where they boiled their coffee and ate hoe-cake and other luxuries.

The right snug hostelry of Mary Lee, a free colored woman and an excellent cook, was the centre of attraction, being thronged with officers, naval and military, all day. Your correspondent and a friend or two were happy enough to sit at a Christian table for almost the first time since leaving Boston, and devour fried pork and eggs, white biscuits, etc. To make our happiness complete, our frames were last night pillowed upon a Northern feather bed. It was a terribly cold night for North Carolina, and we had reason to bless the fate which gave us a warm bed in place of the cold, cheerless old storehouse where most of the boys shivered the night through.

Last evening, after supper, we sat by the cheerful fireside of a North Carolina Unionist, and while we watched the blaze between the jambs, listened with a charmed sense to the tinkle of the tea things as they were washed and set away. Our host, hostess, and two youngest occupied a bed in the warmest corner of the sitting room, " Goff, the Regicide," John and your correspondent slept in the opposite corner. We retired first, but were not too sleepy to watch with thrilling interest the series of comforting preparations before a domestic couple with a baby can retire. The infant was in its happiest mood ; and, while its little limbs were allowed to bask in the firelight, it held a crooning conversation with its father, who assured the offspring that it was a right smart baby and had slept a heap since morning.

It is now high noon of Wednesday. A facetious fellow, one of the heroes of Tarboro', has just informed me that the " object of the expedition (to Plymouth) is accomplished," and that " Plymouth" is to be put upon our banner.

FEBRUARY 8, 1863.

On our way back to Newbern, when, in my last, I gave currency to the rumor that the object of our expedition to Plymouth was accomplished, I only gave echo to a popular mistake. But yesterday noon an order from headquarders, addressed to our right wing, directing us to put ourselves in light marching order, with twenty-four hours' rations of hard tack in our haversacks, gave us a renewed impression of the uncertainty of camp rumors, and told us unmistakably that something was on foot. In the morning Colonel Lee had given us the liberty of the town, and the enthusiasm with which this favor had been received and enjoyed was not a little dampened by the unexpected order, which many of us received while delectating ourselves at the tables spread for us by the natives of Plymouth. What was up ? Where were we to go ? " Into the bush for wood," remarked our always complaisant Quartermaster, " and perhaps a little farther, to stretch your legs, if the roads are not too heavy." As though the heroes of Tarboro' and Goldsboro' needed to have their legs stretched !

We noted suspiciously the twinkle in the eye of the Quartermaster, but fell in at the word of command, and were soon marching out of Plymouth on the " Long Acre Road."

A mile or two out the road forked. Here we left Co. B and half of Co. C to act as picket guards on each avenue. Leaving the Washington road on our right, and soon after our wagons by a pile of dry wood, we found ourselves repeating the old familiar tramp, tramp through the mud and sand and water of North Carolina, past weather-stained but comfortable looking homesteads: past small plantations, through pine woods, through creeks, and over bridges. We were not long in ascertaining the fact that we were on a foraging expedition, and if history should call it a reconnoisance, the misnomer will never restock the stables and storehouses, the bee-hives and hen-roosts, that night depleted along the road of Long Acre. We received an early hint that we were going to capture a lot of bacon, twelve miles out of Plymouth, but if the residents along the road this side that point managed to save their own bacon and things, they certainly had reason to bless their stars. If it would not be considered unsoldierly and too sentimental, your correspondent might feel inclined to deprecate this business of foraging, as it is carried on. It is pitiful to see homes once, perhaps, famed for their hospitality, entered and robbed; even if the robbers respect the code of war. It is not less hard for women and children to be deprived of the means of subsistence because their husbands and sons and brothers are shooting at us from the bush. But war is a great, a terrible, an undiscriminating monster, and no earthly power may stay the ravages of the unleashed brute.

Ten miles from Plymouth we were forced to wade nearly knee deep through a creek one-fourth of a mile wide at the ford. The water was ice-cold, and gave our feet and ankles a pain more intense than I can well describe. At last (about half past ten o'clock) we halted, and were happy to be informed that the object of the expedition was accomplished. The column was near a house. After making somewhat particular inquiries we were informed that we had captured a dozen barrels of pork, and that the chaplain, as a temperance measure, had resolutely knocked in the head of a barrel of sweet cider, but not, however, until a few enterprising fellows had filled their canteens with the delicious beverage. We were now ready to countermarch, and five o'clock this morning found us again at Plymouth, after a night march of twenty-five miles.

But for the risk of being tedious, I would ask the reader to accom-

pany us upon our return, to halt with us at every house and listen to
the voice of disturbed poultry aroused from sleep to die an untimely
death; to see the column halt at every henery, and promptly move
again when the victimized fowls had given utterance to their last
despairing notes; to see donkey carts laden with geese upset in the
creek, and hear the eloquently profane protests of officers and privates
as they again floundered through the ice-water at the long ford. It
was a rough night, but all experience is valuable.

FEBRUARY 9.

We lay still a portion of last night and this forenoon in Albemarle
Sound, on account of fog. This afternoon we were obliged to take
coal, and at nightfall, a mile off Roanoke Island, the fog was again
setting in. We shall probably not reach Newbern until late to-morrow.
This letter will be taken to Roanoke Island, and go from thence to
New York.

NEWBERN, N. C., FEB. 17, 1863.

We are visited occasionally at Newbern by friends from Boston.
Few things are more agreeable to us than the sight of forms and faces
bringing with them airs of home. We scan the dress of a civilian as
something almost *outre* for its singularity. The sight of smooth, white
shirts is positively tantalizing. Among our visitors here have been J.
Thomas Stevenson and wife, father and mother of General Stevenson,
Rev. Mr. Barnard, Rev. Mr. Thompson, of Jamaica Plain, and Rev.
Dr. Lothrop. The latter gentleman preached to the regiment on the
15th. To gaze upon the goodly rotundity of that familiar form was
like being introduced to a slice of Boston, whereof the centre was the
old church and cannon ball in Brattle Square. He favored us with an
admirable discourse from the words, "Keep thy heart with all diligence,
for out of it are the issues of life." No admonition is more needed by
the soldier than that conveyed in this text, and as enforced by the energetic eloquence of Dr. Lothrop. We need frequent reminders of the
justness and greatness of our cause to keep our hearts warmly engaged
in a service so full of sacrifice as this. I fear we have too little of the
martyr-spirit which saves a people, and that the North must make up
in numbers and treasure what it lacks in the heroic spirit of the fathers
of the Revolution. If our nice young gentlemen at home hope to keep
clear of this scrape, I fear they will be disappointed.

Among our visitors from Boston, I should have mentioned Sergeant

Wheelwright, who came out as supercargo of the schooner Fry. The reception which his friends in the regiment extended to him was of the most touching description. After numerous affectionate embraces, he was invited to take a drink—of quinine! This being declined, hard tack and salt horse were severally pressed upon him with an urgent hospitality difficult to be refused. Upon our late expedition from Plymouth (named the *ham-fat*), Sergeant Wheelwright acted as orderly for Colonel Lee, and showed himself a forager of great natural ability. As we witnessed him first mounted upon a dashing mule, and then a fleet horse, we could hardly persuade ourselves that he had not profited by the rich experiences of Tarboro' and Goldsboro'.

Among the few deaths which have recently occurred in the regiment is that of private Hopkinson, of Company F, who died of typhoid fever. He was a graduate of Harvard College, and one of the brightest intellects in the regiment. A few years ago he was temporarily connected with the Boston Advertiser. His remains have been embalmed, and will be sent North.

We are beginning to feel the breath of spring. Dandelions are commencing to bloom in Newbern, and wild onions are springing up over our parade ground. At night the neighboring swamps are vocal with the voices of frogs.

We are to have a dramatic entertainment with which to celebrate the anniversary of Washington's birth-day, provided, of course, we are allowed to remain in Newbern. At present our brigade is a divided one, the Connecticut 10th and the Massachusetts 24th being a part of the great Southern expedition. General Stevenson is with the 10th and 24th. The remaining regiment of our brigade, the Rhode Island 5th, is with us at Newbern.

----

NEWBERN, N. C., FEB. 28, 1863.

We celebrated Washington's birthday on the evening of the 23d by a *bal masque* in the barracks of Companies D and E. The affair crowned and surpassed all our previous efforts in this line, and was universally decided to be a big thing. The barracks, which had recently been whitewashed, were united by the removal of a partition, and formed a saloon one hundred and twenty feet in length. The fronts of the bunks were covered with shelter tents depending like curtains. To these at proper intervals were attached scrolls with green borders bearing the names of the captains and lieutenants of the regiment. More conspicuously appeared the names of Colonel Lee and staff, General Stevenson, of our brigade, General Wessells, of our division, and General Foster, chief of this army corps. At the head of the saloon was erected a platform carpeted with rubber blankets. Back of this was suspended a large American flag, with the name of Washington upon a scroll. Upon other scrolls appeared the date of his birth and the words " First in war," &c. Midway of the barracks was a graceful canopy of flags, and at various other points the national colors were appropriately disposed to heighten the general effect. Our well-burnished rifles were crossed on the front of the bunks, and rayed from centers on the walls. Chandeliers, beautifully trimmed with green and moss, lighted up the long room and its decorations, and gave the apartment an appearance of real magnificence. It even surpassed the most sanguine expectations of those who had industriously labored upon the decorations. Such was the appearance of the barracks alone ; but when later in the evening they were crowded with people wearing the varied and grotesque costumes of the occasion, and the uniforms of a large number of officers, the scene was more brilliant than I can describe.

But the chief feature of the occasion was the presence of General Foster, General Wessells, and a large number of officers from various regiments in this department, all of whom were pleased to warmly commend the taste and enterprise of the 44th boys. It is needless to say that the presence of our distinguished visitors was enthusiastically recognized by us.

The following was the order of dances :—

1. March and Sicilian Circle . . . . . . Lee's Quickstep.
2. Quadrille . . . . . . . . Sullivan's Double Quick.
3. Les Lancers . . . . . . . . Richardson's March.
4. Contra . . . . . . . . . Skittletop Gallop.
5. Polka Redowa . . . . . . . . Odiorne's Choice.
6. Quadrille . . . . . . . . . Surgeon's Call.
7. Polka . . . . . . . . Mary Lee's Delight.
8. Contra . . . . . . . . . Stebbins's Reel.

INTERMISSION.

Waltz—Varsovienne—Schottische.

9. Quadrille . . . . . . . . . Ham Fat Man.
10. Waltz . . . . . . . . . . Pas de Seul.
11. Quadrille . . . . . . . . Dismal Swamp Promenade.
12. Contra . . . . . . . . . Our Friends at Home.
13. Polka Quadrille . . . . . . . Long Acre Gallop.
14. Quadrille . . . . . . . . . Dug-out Race.
15. Military do. . . . . . . . . Newell's March.

Here is the managerial card:

### GRAND MASQUERADE BALL.

Sir:—The pleasure of your company, with ladies, is respectfully solicited at a Grand Bal Masque to be given under the auspices of the 44th Regimental Dramatic Association, at the Barracks of Companies D and E, on

### MONDAY EVENING, FEB. 23. 1863.

The management desire to state that nothing will be left undone to render it the party of the season.

#### FLOOR MANAGERS.

Willard Howard.                    J. B. Rice,                    Harry T. Reed.

#### COMMITTEE OF ARRANGEMENTS.

| | | |
|---|---|---|
| Sergeant G. L. Tripp, | . . . . . . . . . | Company D. |
| "      H. A. Homer, | . . . . . . . . | "      E. |
| Corporal Z. T. Haines, | . . . . . . . . | "      D. |
| "      J. B. Gardner, | . . . . . . . . . | "      D. |
| "      J. W. Cartwright, | . . . . . . . | "      E. |
| "      M. E. Boyd, | . . . . . . . . | "      D. |
| "      C. E. Tucker, | . . . . . . . . | "      E. |
| Private F. A. Sayer, | . . . . . . . . | "      D. |
| "      H. Howard, | . . . . . . . . . | "      D. |
| "      J. H. Waterman, Jr., | . . . . . . . | "      D. |
| "      H. Bradish, | . . . . . . . . . | "      E. |
| "      C. H. Demeritt, | . . . . . . . . | "      D. |
| "      D. Howard, | . . . . . . . . . | "      D. |
| "      E. L. Hill, | . . . . . . . . | "      A. |

In order to defray the expenses, Tickets will be placed at 10 cents each, to be procured of the Managers. No tickets sold at the door. Visitors are expected to appear *en costume.*

Music by the New Berne Quadrille Band, five pieces.

The Management desire to express their sincere thanks to the Officers of this Regiment for the many favors granted by them in aid of this undertaking.

The hall will be appropriately decorated.

The Newbern Quadrille Band, composed of *discolored* young gentlemen, did not distinguish itself; but our own regimental band, under Major Babcock,—which, by the way, has received its splendid new instruments,—came to the rescue gallantly, and added largely to the *eclat* of the affair, which, by the way, was *pecuniarily* successful, leaving us funds which will enable us to produce in good time an original opera, and one expected to contain several local and personal hits. But of that hereafter.

The following deaths have recently occurred in the regiment:

Geo. B. Young, Co. G, malarious fever.

Charles A. Bradt, Co. C, malarious fever.

E. N. Fuller, Co. A, measles.

James S. Gilmore, Co. K, diptheria and lung fever.

Sergt. Charles Harwood, Co. I, diptheria.

This month fifteen men have been discharged for disability. The general health of the regiment, however, is quite good—better than it was a short time ago ; but experience is convincing all concerned that our miserably pinched up barracks are a fruitful cause of disease. The regiments in tents are the healthiest ones.

The Boston regiment of colored men has excited much interest here. Some of our best men have accepted commissions in it. Among these are Lieut. Hartwell, Sergts. James and Russell, of Co. F. We shall part with these men with great regret, and at the same time give them a hearty Godspeed in their brave and self-sacrificing undertaking. There is no warmer friend of the Massachusetts 54th regiment than Col. Lee ; and the best evidence of the fact is in the cheerful alacrity which he shows in supplying it with officers from the best men of his own command. I understand that Gen. Foster favors the scheme of recruiting regiments of colored men. Several items of regimental news must lie over.

———

NEWBERN, N. C., MARCH 4, 1863.

My last letter contained a brief account of a Washington birth-day ball in our barracks, but the hasty description I was then obliged to give conveyed a very inadequate idea of the brilliancy of the subject, and will be quite unsatisfactory to those who were present. I cannot remember a ball-room which presented a finer effect in its decorations than ours. It was remarkable to observe what a little taste and industry were able to accomplish with our limited means, not only as respects the decorations, but in the costumes and characters assumed. The young women who had stunned all beholders at previous masquerades, appeared with augmented charms. Some were doubtless outstripped by others, but I shall this time avoid invidious comparisons. The " Albino Family," with head-dresses of frayed ropes, was an exceedingly clever take-off of Barnum's curious beings at the Aquarial Gardens. Deacon Doolittle, of Vermont, who had come down to Newbern to gratify himself with the spectacle of young men bleeding for their country, was one of the richest impersonations of the evening. The old man was deeply surprised to see young ladies smoking cigars, and averred that such a thing was unheard of when he was a young man. Deacon Doolittle got interested in Deacon Foster, and the two were seen arm-in-arm. The white woolly locks and limp of the latter deacon were unmistakable in the throng. Deacon Doolittle's humanitarian character having got noised about among the managers, the old man was invited to the platform, from which he made an edifying address, at last bringing down the house by kissing a gun which he held in his hand.

Among other assumptions were those of a member of the Howard street blackleg fraternity, "The Press," a harlequin, several devils, &c., &c. "The Press" was clad in newspapers, the Sunday Herald being conspicuous among a great variety of enterprising journals displayed in the costume. Several rollicking sailors and dashing cavalry officers gave variety to the costumes and added life to the scene. The little brigadier of Company A was admirably made up, and the character was sustained in a manner truly artistic. The same may be said of the little Continental brigadier of Company E, the Indian, of the same company, the Turk, of Company F, and Miss Columbia, of Company C, who, being the " Gem of the Ocean," was observed to be on intimate terms with one of the sailors. Some of our friends will have the pleasure of examining pictures of several of these characters, and will thus obtain a better idea of their appearance than it is possible for me to give in words, even if I should undertake the hopeless task.

Last Wednesday, the 25th, witnessed a grand review of the troops at Newbern. Our friends may be pleased to know that the 44th Regiment was generally acknowledged to be second to no regiment in the field for the excellence of its marching and general appearance. The review was witnessed by a large number of spectators, including many ladies in carriages and on horseback.

Day before yesterday Companies F and B, Captains Storrow and Griswold, were sent out to do picket duty a few miles up the railroad.

The last death in our regiment was that of Otis S. Merrill, of Company C, who died of measles. Nearly fifty are on the sick list. There are but few cases of malarious fever among our men, but the Massachusetts 51st has suffered quite severely from it. That regiment is soon to commence garrison duty at Beaufort and Fort Macon, the Paradise of this department. The 44th will probably soon do provost marshal duty in Newbern.

NEWBERN, N. C., MARCH 14, 1863.

The peaceful quiet of our life at Newburn was to-day interrupted by an attack from the rebels. Gen. Foster had arranged to celebrate the day in a manner becoming the anniversary of the capture of New-

bern. But a grand march in review and other *et ceteras* were unexpectedly substituted by salutes with shot and shell from a brigade of
rebels on the eastern shore of the Neuse, who made an early attack
upon our outpost on that shore. This outpost force, which is stationed
directly opposite the camp of our regiment, consisted of the New York
92nd regiment, strongly entrenched near the shore. Previous to the
attack, the rebel General (Pettigrew) is reported to have sent in
several demands for a surrender, which were promptly refused. The
rebels then commenced a vigorous fire of grape and canister, which
passed harmlessly over the heads of the little garrison, and beat the
waters of the Neuse into foam. An occasional shell from the rebel
lines came over the river and lodged upon our parade ground; and
groups of spectators from our regiment, standing upon the shore, were
admonished not to present too conspicuous a mark for the enemy's
artillery. After a while, the rebels, observing the inefficacy of their
fire, as the story goes about camp, attempted to carry our works by
storm, but without result, save in a serious loss from the volleys which
met their approach. In the meanwhile, several of our gunboats were
doing good service by landing shells at proper places, and feeling up
and down shore with their iron fingers. Several field batteries were
also set at work on either side of our barracks, and by noon the rebel
artillery was silenced.

Of course the air is full of rumors, to wit: immense force of rebels
on every side; rebel generals swear they will dine at the Gaston House
to-morrow; pickets driven in or captured on the Neuse and Trent roads;
Beaufort and Roanoke captured; the railroad seized; more fighting
to-night, &c. &c. That our pickets have been disturbed is doubtless
true. Artillery and infantry have been sent out on the great roads,
and over the Neuse the picket force is augmented, and great vigilance
is for some good reason exercised. I shall not be able to send you
later advices by this departure. We are not much frightened; and, if
we have got to fight the rebels, have no objections to doing so once
with the advantages on our side. I allude to gunboats, plenty of
ammunition, rifle pits, &c., and no long marches.

I enclose herewith the libretto of an opera written and produced
by members of our regiment. If you will reprint it, it may amuse
some of our friends in Boston, although its best points are more
apparent to the members of the regiment than to anybody else. You
will not find the music. That was improvised and selected, and very
many appropriate airs and witticisms were introduced in places not

indicated in the printed text. It has been publicly produced three times before large audiences (two long barracks being full each time), including officers of the highest rank in this Department. Thursday night Gen. Foster and staff, with his wife and nearly all the Northern ladies now resident in Newbern, were present. With the body of the house filled by officers in full uniform, opera has rarely been honored by a more brilliant audience. We had a spacious stage, an act-drop, and other scenery, foraged from an old theatre in Newbern, some scenery painted by our own artists, a profusion of flags and green decorations, and a beautiful tableau with blue-lights to close with. The orchestra, under the lead of Mr. Hooke, played splendidly, and with a truly theatrical effect. Altogether, our distinguished auditors expressed themselves not only remarkably pleased with our efforts, but greatly surprised at what we had been able to accomplish under the circumstances of our position. Last night we gave an entertainment to the invalid guards of the Connecticut 10th and the Massachusetts 24th, the two detached regiments of our brigade, and one hundred men from the Rhode Island 5th. A thousand copies of the libretto have been printed, and their sale has added a handsome amount to the charitable fund of the regiment.

MARCH 15.

The night was peaceful. Our extra pickets have come in, and the rebels are believed to have skedaddled. It is probable that their main purpose was to capture our outpost on the east side of the Neuse, but, failing in this, have retreated. The rebels will always find Newbern a hot place.

---

WASHINGTON, N. C., March 16, 1863.

We bid fair to get the name of the expeditionary regiment of this department. You will observe by the date of this letter that we have again pulled up stakes at Newbern, and moved to Washington, at the head of Pamlico Sound. Our friends will want an explanation of this new movement. My last letter mentioned an unsuccessful rebel attack on our outpost on the easterly side of the Neuse. We were afterwards informed by negroes and deserters that seven hundred rebels were engaged in this attack, and that eight thousand were at the same time moving down on the Trent road, where they were promptly held in check by infantry and artillery sent out by General Foster. It is quite probable that these figures were not far from correct. That the rebels

were in large force at Kinston has been well understood ever since our
return from the Goldsboro' raid, and they probably thought to make an
easy conquest of the little force over the Neuse, well knowing that
it would form a very pretty little celebration of the anniversary of
the capture of Newbern. But failing in this project, as well as in
their attempt to plant batteries with which to shell the town, the rebel
forces withdrew. But it was a matter of some doubt with General Foster whether the rebels would return to Kinston without attempting to
accomplish something in this direction. He therefore determined to
strengthen the garrison at Washington by sending hither our regiment,
minus companies F and B, on picket, and here we are. We left Newbern last evening by the fine new little steamer Escort, and after a
pleasant trip arrived here this afternoon. We came up to the wharf
with music and flying colors, creating by our advent no little sensation
among the soldiers and contrabands who came dancing down to the
river in flocks. The afternoon sun was shining briskly, and Washington presented a very lively and attractive air. We find eight companies
of the Massachusetts 27th here, two companies of the North Carolina
regiment, a company of cavalry and a company of artillery. The town
is admirably protected by earthworks, block houses and a formidable
fort, to say nothing of three gunboats in the stream. Neverthless, a
rebel attack seems to be anticipated. Colonel Lee, of our regiment, in
command of the detached brigade, formed by the Massachusetts 44th
and the Rhode Island 5th, assumes command of this post. Tonight
we bivouac a little west of the town upon the famous Grist plantation.
We are occupying shelter tents for the first time, and find them "quite
bully." The rapidity with which our canvas village assumed shape was
amazing. The boys are assembled about the bivouac fires in high sport,
or reading or writing by the light of candles within the tents. Colonel
Lee has delighted all hearts by taking possession of the Grist mansion
as his headquarters. The loyalty of its proprietor is said to be of such
an uncertain character that Colonel Lee has decided to put a little
wholesome restriction upon his future movements. His house and
grounds are the most elegant we have seen in North Carolina, and his
cellar is said to be well stored with apple-jack. Grist himself is a fat,
impudent looking specimen of the race of secesh.

MARCH 17.

While we were standing about the fires this morning waiting for our
coffee, we received a hurried order to strike tents. We had no doubt
that, in consequence of important news from the pickets, a march was

in contemplation, but were soon agreeably disappointed to ascertain that we were only required to pitch our tents so as to form company streets. Upon this job we then entered with alacrity.

Grist (who is profanely misnamed by the soldiers) packed up his goods this morning preparatory to moving to his suburban residence outside our lines; but Colonel Lee decided that he couldn't dispense with his fascinating society at this juncture, especially as Governor Stanley's passport is no longer valuable to Grist or any other of the Governor's rebel favorites. Grist submitted philosophically. His mansion looms up temptingly among the trees near the right of our line. The place, I am told, figured in Porte Crayon's North Carolina sketches ; but the mansion has been renovated since then. It has doubtless been one of many hospitable homes in Washington, which place is said to have been famed for its hospitality.

This afternoon we were startled from our siestas by the metallic crack of rifled cannon on one of the gunboats. It was a charming sound,— scarcely less so than the dulcet strains of the 44th band, which at the present moment is discoursing "Departed Days" at Colonel Lee's headquarters. They were feeling for rebels in the woods on the south side of the river. Scouts sent over the bridge last night and to-day report the presence of the enemy's pickets and intrenchments two or three miles up the road.

MARCH 18.

No further sign of the enemy. After spending most of a very warm day in listlessness, we were marched through the town this evening for a dress parade with the 27th, upon the spot where we bivouaced last fall. The dust was intolerable, and the "expedition" was generally regarded as a non-paying one. It afforded us, however, a good view of the town and its inhabitants. The female portion of the latter are not remarkable for smiling countenances. As a rule they are not lovely, being either podgy, with turn-up noses, or bony and forlorn. They talk through their noses.

MARCH 20.

Your correspondent assisted in the performance of picket duty last night. The weather was terribly severe. For some reason or other an attack was momentarily expected, and we were kept upon the *qui vive*. When we returned this morning, benumbed and drenched to the skin with rain, we found the infantry all behind the earthworks ready for action. It is now night, but there are no signs of the enemy.

WASHINGTON, N. C., MARCH 20, 1863.

Our late exposure upon picket duty, and the continued rain, induced our officers to mercifully permit us to leave our shelter tents, and occupy houses in town, so to-night we find ourselves happy in the enjoyment of excellent shelter and warm fires. What a contrast with our situation last night out on the Tarboro' road, drenched to the skin and chilled to the centre! The liberty of the town has enabled us to fortify ourselves with such dainties as ham and eggs, milk, &c., and we are now as comfortable as heart could wish. Better than all, we are not likely to be disturbed to-night, for our cavalry scouts bring intelligence of the withdrawal of the rebels from this vicinity.

Near where our shelter tents are pitched is the humble domicil of Aunt Fanny and family, members of the patriarchal household of Grist. Fanny's fireside was a great centre of attraction, and about it the soldiers crowded in scores to escape the rain, against which cotton houses proved a slim protection. Aunt Fanny is of a retiring disposition, and it required the exercise of unusual energy on her part to keep one little place at the fire for herself and children. She must have shared our joy, but for another reason, when we were ordered to take up our abode in town. While we remained in her vicinity, all she could do was to fortify herself with snuff, of which she is a veteran " dipper." Our presence must have caused a large consumption of this consoling article. She transferred the snuff from a tin box to her mouth with a sweet gum wood stick, which she used like a tooth brush, and then left the handle sticking out of her mouth. Aunt Fanny afforded me the first opportunity I ever had of witnessing the operation of " dipping," and I am thus particular in my reference to this classic custom, which is said to prevail among the white women as well as the black ones at the South. Aunt Fanny's sombre face and the protruding handle of the gum stick would form a fit subject for the pencil of Porte Crayon. While I witnessed, with a twinge of sympathy, Aunt Fanny's patient sufferance of the invasion of her castle, I could not but wish that some good fairy would suddenly endow her with the momentum and muscular power of the shoulder-hitting *Charity*, empress of the Newbern washerwomen, who submits to no nonsense, but lays about her, right and left, according to the number of those who provoke her just wrath by unseemly liberties.

MARCH 21.

Last night the Thespians of the 27th Regiment performed " The Irish Tutor " and " Michael Earle." They have fitted up a little theatre, and furnished it with an act drop, scenery, &c., of their own painting. Our own dramatic corps are quite unhappy to find Washington without a suitable opera house. It is proposed when we get back to Newbern to produce Dr. Jones's "Solon Shingle," if the public demand for more opera is not too clamorous. The musical world will be glad to know that the organs of our principal singers are as yet unaffected by the severe trials of picket duty; a fact the more noticeable, perhaps, considering that those organs have not been lubricated with whisky rations from first to last of our severe trials as soldiers. It won't do for soldiers to murmur in public, but you can fancy our feelings! It is assumed by our naval men here that the rebels have two gunboats up the Tar River. This is probably correct. The building of a gunboat at Tarboro' was among the supposed reasons for our attempted expedition to that place last November. Very little fear of them, however, exists. It is imagined by some that the rebels will come down upon this place in scows. That route would please us. We find the colored population here quite fearful of an attack, and many of them with their effects packed up preparatory to a hurried removal to boats. Among these is Henrietta, a very nice young woman, the slave of a Unionist, who cooks excellent dinners for a few of us hungry fellows, in a snug, white-washed cabin at the east end of the town. Henrietta is as neat, intelligent and lady-like as the average of white women. Her bondage, if such it can be called, sits lightly upon her; but she has no sympathy for rebels, and like many others here, severely denounces the suttlers who, for the sake of making money, furnish the secessionists of this region with food and clothing. Henrietta rejoices in the possession of an excellent cow, a *rara avis* in North Carolina. The peach trees in her garden have put on their pink dresses, and the robins, wooed by their fragrance, are trapped and murdered by Henrietta for her table. I caught the lady in this slaughtering business, and found her a little nervous about the law touching her case.

A party of us strayed into the old town hall to-day. The official papers and books were strewn all over the building without the slightest appearance of any attempt at preservation or order. While wandering through the maze, an officer attached to the permanent garrison of the place appeared before us, and sharply ordered us away from the premises. We course obeyed, but thought his exercise of authority was in poor keeping with the utter neglect and destruction which had already been allowed to mark the building and its contents.

MARCH 22, 1863.

Went to a negro church to-day in an old building not long since used as a theatre, the fresco and gilding still remaining about the proscenium. The preacher and his chief men and women sat upon the stage, the bulk of the audience, including several soldiers, in front. The singing was congregational, and line by line, as it was read by the preacher. It was horrible. The praying and preaching better appealed to the emotions. We certainly were not unmoved by the earnest petition in behalf of the " soldiers of the North who had given them their liberty," by the prayers for the welfare of our friends at home, and for victory over our enemies. The sermon was an invocation for watchfulness, with copious illustrations from military experience. It was rich in funny logic and quaint grammar.

After a three days' equinoctial storm, the sun is out cheeringly this afternoon.

MARCH 23, 1863.

There is a boat in from Newbern this morning, and the indications are that our ten days' absence is to be indefinitely extended. All the companies but D and H, who are housed near our camp-ground, are ordered back to the shelter tents. " Bully for D and H" is the general sentiment.

Horace P. Tuttle, the soldier-astronomer of our regiment, has been appointed assistant paymaster in the navy. He has not fully decided to accept the unexpected and unsolicited honor, and we hope he may remain with his many friends of the 44th through its term of service.

I think I have not mentioned in this or my previous letter from Washington that but eight of our companies are here. Companies B and F, Captains Griswold and Storrow, were left behind doing picket duty on the railroad a few miles above Newbern.

———

WASHINGTON, N. C., MARCH 24, 1863.

We are not much in love with this Washington, N. C. It seems too much like " some banquet hall deserted." We suspect it of insalubrity. We don't like " the folks." We shall be glad when we strike tents. But while we remain here we propose to avail ourselves of all mitigating circumstances. Last evening, John Smith, banjoist, came to our quarters at the Pamlee mansion. His instrument was made of an old sieve and a pine stick, but in volume and sweetness of tone, I don't remember to have heard it surpassed. Of course it set all the niggers to dancing, especially our old friend and favorite, West Williams, who earned new laurels in the light fantastic. John Smith, besides being a splendid banjoist, has a voice like a robin.

To-day the lines have been open, and the women of the suburbs have been thronging into town to buy a little sugar, coffee, snuff, &c., especially snuff. Our friend Grist has at last been permitted to go outside the lines. He doesn't attempt to disguise a degree of sympathy with the Southern cause, but his outward conduct towards us has been gentlemanly.

Contrabands report a large rebel force (seven thousand) within seven miles of Washington, one day last week; and that they were restrained from advancing on the place by hearing that the garrison was reinforced. If this is true, "the object of the expedition is accomplished," and we may expect to return to Newbern very soon. One of the officers of the permanent garrison here has taken a Southern woman for a wife. They are our next door neighbors. As we see them together, planting flowers in the door-yard, we fancy we might become reconciled even to Washington, N. C., under such circumstances. There is a call now upon the gardening skill of the regiment, and some of the boys have voluntarily ornamented the vicinity of their shelter-tents with plants in full bloom.

Washington, N. C., in its palmy days, is described as "a hard old place." It was a slave market of some consequence, and the population consumed a good deal of "ardent spirits," according to the authority of a venerable "aunty" who lives in a cabin attached to our quarters. Street duels were a common affair. An election was considered tame without two or three attendant rows and stabbings. The poor white people left behind here, and even those of respectable appearance, are unable to read or write. They considered it unlawful to send their children to school—so says a decent looking woman whose husband is an unwilling soldier in the rebel army. The more we learn of the despicable social condition of the South, the stronger appears the need of the purification which, in the Providence of God, comes of the fire and the sword.

MARCH 25.

While Company K was quartered in town they were directly opposite a house inhabited with others by a comely young woman, who so excited the admiration of a susceptible young man in the company that he was impelled to send her a love missive. It was in good set terms, smelling strongly of "The Ready Letter-Writer," but the young lady was so little moved by its elegance, that she returned the note with a resentful addendum, threatening to tell the Colonel, and expressing a wish to have no communication with her "enemies."

A gunboat came in from Newbern last night, increasing the fleet to four. We have a fine bracing air to-day, and the health of the regiment is excellent. We are also made happy by a mail from the North containing bills of lading, which means boxes for us at Newbern.

I learn to-day that Plymouth has again been menaced by the rebels, but that the prompt arrival of reinforcements saved the place. Gen. Foster is never caught napping. An increasing confidence is entertained for his generalship.

----

WASHINGTON, N. C., MARCH 30, 1863.

Yesterday completed the first seven months of our service as volunteer soldiers, dating from the time we went into camp at Readville as a full, organized regiment. Whether our term of service commenced on the 29th of August or on the 12th of September, when we were formally mustered into service, is not yet definitely announced; but we incline to the opinion that we shall be held for nine months from the latter date. It has been rumored that we are to be detained for nine months from the time that we received marching orders, late in October, but we have little fear of that. It is needless to say that almost every man in the regiment is looking fondly forward to his emancipation from the restraints, deprivations, and hardships of military life to the reunion of hearts and the enjoyment of home comforts.

Yesterday I again attended worship at a colored church, and afterward proceeded with the congregation to a baptism in the river. The sacred ordinance was characterized by entire decorum. The blacks here, who comprise a great majority of the resident population of Washington, are extremely fervent in their prayers for the success of the Northern cause, and rightly attribute their enlarged liberty to the presence of our soldiers. They are a more intelligent and orderly population than can be shown in the foreign precincts of our great cities. The only black man here who disturbs the peace is "Crazy Willis." He perambulates the streets incessantly, swearing that the war must be stopped, and that no more Yankees shall be killed. His harangues present a curious blending of profanity and pious exhortation. He was formerly a preacher of more than usual fluency. He is a very unpopular member of society, his black brethren not giving him credit for much insanity.

Gen. Foster and staff arrived here this morning, and reinforcements are said to be close by. Whether this means additional defence or another expedition I cannot say at this writing.

P. M. This forenoon a scouting party, consisting of Companies A and G, with a few cavalrymen and one piece of artillery, crossed the bridge and proceeded up the road about two miles, when they were suddenly arrested by rebels in ambush. Company G were acting as skirmishers, and advanced to within a few feet of the rebels' hiding place before receiving their fire. The result was disastrous. Three of Co. G's men were brought down and left upon the ground at the narrow defile where the rebels were posted. Capt. James Richardson, of Co. A, received two bullets in the left arm. No bones were broken. Upon receiving the fire, our men were ordered to seek cover on either side of the road, which they did until they deemed it safe to rally and return to town.

Those left dead or wounded are Orderly Sergt. Hobart, Corporal Lawrence and John Leonard, all of Co. G. Corporal King of the same company was slightly wounded by a buck-shot in the back of the head. Lieut. Odiorne's clothes were riddled with bullets and buck-shot, as were those of Corporal Priest. One of the latter's hands was grazed by a projectile. Others had equally narrow escapes.

March 31.

We spent last night behind the breastworks, sleeping in our blankets and watching by turns It rained almost incessantly, and we were drenched to the skin. Toward morning we were allowed to spend an hour in one of the block-houses with the boys of Co. B, Mass. 27th; but we passed most of this forenoon in the mud behind the breastworks, with no other consolation than coffee and hard tack. The gunboats and fort were firing into the woods all night, to prevent the erection of batteries. At daylight our attention was arrested by sharp musketry firing over the river. We afterwards learned that a battalion of North Carolina troops, under Capt. Lyon, had been sent over to prevent the erection of rebel batteries at Point Rodman, a short distance below, and that they succeeded in their purpose by smart skirmishing, in which several of their men were wounded.

April 1.

The rebels lay low yesterday, and the night was peaceful; but before morning they succeeded in planting one or more formidable batteries commanding the river below, and this morning they opened on the town and our gunboats. To make matters worse, a strong west wind was driving the water out of the river, leaving our gunboats aground. This left the Hull badly exposed to the guns of the first rebel fort, and they played into her in a lively manner, dismounting two of her guns and wounding two or three of her men. The guns of the Hull, however, were not idle, but blazed away until her ammunition was exhausted. The Louisiana and Eagle were also busy during the day, but to-night no guns are heard on either side. Numerous rebel projectiles of the Whitworth pattern came into the town, but did no damage to speak of. The wind has abated, the water has risen on the river, and the gunboats are afloat again. Dispatch boats succeeded in running the blockade yesterday and to-day.

APRIL 2.

Last night was quiet, but we busied ourselves in strengthening our defences. There are well-founded rumors of gunboats and reinforcements below the rebel forts, and distant firing is heard from down the river, suggesting the probability of other rebel forts farther down. A rebel flag is descried down the river, but otherwise there is very little to be seen or heard of the enemy. The videttes think the rebels are skedaddling, and the boys are in high spirits.

Yesterday our pickets over the bridge learned from the enemy's pickets that the wounded men of Co. G, who were left in the hands of the enemy on the 31st, are doing well. None were killed. Orderly Hobart, who was the most seriously hurt, was shot through one of the lungs.

In consequence of the weakness of our garrison, General Foster has organized a battalion of blacks to assist us behind the earthworks. We have no such enthusiastic soldiers in the department as they. They begged the privilege of having guns placed in their hands, and almost quarrelled for the preference. They swear they will sell their lives as dearly as possible. We are indebted, by the way, to a colored servant of Captain Kendall, who went beyond the lines the other day, for information of great value.

Yesterday a boat containing half a dozen persons was seen to cross the river a few hundred yards west of the extreme left of our line of earthworks, and land upon a point running from this shore. A six-pounder in the block-house was trained upon them, and sent them scattering in double quick time. Some of us have a troublesome suspicion that the boat's crew were deserters or contrabands. If they were rebels, their audacity is unexplainable.

To-day one of our videttes reports seeing a man suspended by the neck to an apple-tree beyond our lines. He made a careful examination with a glass, and saw a rebel officer and several privates engaged in lowering and dragging away the body, which was probably that of a man suspected of disloyalty to the rebel cause. Such is rebel justice.

APRIL 3.

Another quiet night last night, although in the evening the principal rebel fort down the river fired several shots at what we surmised was a transport or gunboat coming up. Our conjecture was probably correct, as to-day we learn that fresh supplies of ammunition had been received. We are told that three regiments and two gunboats, from Newbern, are a few miles down the river, also more rebel batteries, and one of them so buried in the ground as to be unassailable by anything save mortars. Yesterday the block-house on our extreme right was a particular mark for rebel cannon. Very little damage was done, but a large gun taken from a gunboat and placed at the block-house was believed to be doing a good business. Some of the large rebel guns near the shore have been withdrawn, and one knocked out of position. Our gunboats have been firing at frequent intervals, all day to-day, although the rebels opened the ball in the morning.

P. M. We hear that *five* gunboats are down the river, and that while they were engaging the rebel batteries, a dispatch schooner sailed up past them. A contraband who escaped from the rebels to-day, reports that we have killed " a right smart of 'em." This is very likely. A more uncertain report is that of a rebel flag of truce asking for time to bury their dead.

A vidette stationed near our block-house ventured a little too far out to-day, and exchanged shots with some rebels near a point of woods. He saw a lot of horses, mules and wagons under cover of the woods.

We are beginning to ask, " How much longer is this thing to go on ?" What is the purpose of the rebels ? To keep away reinforcements and provisions until they force us into a bloodless capitulation, or until they concentrate troops enough to carry our breastworks by storm ? Or do they hope to draw troops enough from Newbern to leave that place exposed to capture ? Or do they merely propose keeping us busy, to prevent us from sending any more troops from North Carolina for the reinforcement of the army in the Department of the South. Time only will show. We have no great apprehensions concerning the result. Our confidence in General Foster is firm and unabated. His timely presence here we regard as little less than providential.

We are still stationed close to the entrenchments which encircle the town, in shelter tents and block-houses. Company D is fortunately quartered with Company B, of the Massachusetts 27th, in block-house No. 1 and its out-buildings. We are under great obligation to them for their obliging hospitality. Their long experience has qualified them to give us many useful lessons in camp life. We watch their culinary operations with great interest, and are not a little tantalized by the sight of warm bread, flap-jacks, fried fish, &c., especially as we are now chiefly confined to hard-tack and miserable coffee.

Our black recruits are industriously drilling in marching and the manual. The favorite servants of our company, whom some of my readers will remember by the names of America and West, are exhibiting their talents as drill officers, to excellent effect. Our colored recruits are already winning golden opinions for their soldierly qualities. Our most bitter negropholists admit that they will *fight*, and one of their sincere haters has been detailed to officer them. Some of the poor fellows lie behind the breastworks with a spelling book in one hand and a musket in the other.

APRIL 4.

Last night was tolerably quiet, although the gunboats occasionally woke the echoes. This morning a gunboat passed the rebel batteries, and came to anchor opposite the town. She was not fired at, but eight rebel guns were seen in position. There is a growing suspicion that the rebels have abandoned the siege.

9 P. M.

"A growing suspicion" has not been sustained. A reconnoisance was attempted to-day with a view of sounding the rebels in the vicinity of the battery on the point, but our boats were fired upon, and another artillery duel occupied the afternoon. We were again ordered behind the breastworks, but to-night are permitted to share the comfortable quarters of Company B, 27th. When we get home we propose to print in the Herald a card of thanks to Company B, after the style of the boys of Extinguisher 20, to the boys of Cataract 11—"We owe you one."

APRIL 5.

The quiet of last night and this forenoon has been unbroken by the sound of guns; but this afternoon the Sunday stillness is interrupted by

the solemn boom of heavy artillery down the river. Whether it pro-
ceeds from the rebel forts or our gunboats we do not know. Yesterday
it was rumored that the spades were collected and sent down the river
to be used in intrenching our reinforcements held back by the blockade.
Certain it is, we could get no spades for our own use last night. It
was rumored yesterday that the rebels were feeling about Newbern.

APRIL 6.

The rebels have been throwing up additional earthworks down the
river, and seem to have entered upon the siege in earnest. The smoke
of their bivouac fires increases from night to night, and it is highly
probable that they are receiving reinforcements of infantry.

APRIL 8.

An attack was strongly expected night before last, and a heavy picket force was stationed all along our line of defence. In the edge of the
evening a boat with two black fugitives came down the river. They
had escaped from the rebels, but brought us very little useful intelligence regarding their numbers or position. Yesterday a black boy
came in from the enemy's lines with large stories about their force, size
of their guns, &c. The rebel general had made his men a speech, and
they were to attack us yesterday morning. General Foster thinks the
boy was *sent* in, and so has quartered him in the guard house. At all
events, the rebels did not appear this morning. In fact they seem inclined to give us plenty of time, which, of course, we are improving to
the best of our ability, by the erection of traverses, additional breastworks and forts. We have also placed upon the top of our earthworks
three or four thicknesses of turf. The block-house where our company
is stationed is on the extreme left of our line of defence, and is conse-
quently most exposed to an attack from up the river, which is among
the strong probabilities of this siege. Flat boats and steamers provided
with guns and armor of cotton bales are reported above, and are expected to join in the attack when the land forces get ready, provided
they escape certain formidable river obstructions intended for their
benefit.

We are strongly posted, but are few in numbers. Our entire garrison, armed contrabands included, scarcely amounts to two thousand
men. The gunboats have failed in silencing the rebel shore batteries,
and we know not but the river is substantially blockaded. Of course
we shall soon be short of provisions. Our chief ground of hope for re-
lease, in case the rebel attack is longer deferred, is in the arrival of
forces from Newbern, or from Suffolk overland. General Foster was

looking for aid from General Dix yesterday. Of course the aid did not arrive,—it never does.

We had a strong picket out again last night, but everything was remarkably quiet. Our incorrigible Jo says the pickets of the two forces were so near together that they distinctly heard each other eating hard tack! To-day the rebel pickets on the north side are reported to have disappeared, but this morning the rebels on the south side of the river are sending their Whitworth "cucumbers" into town in a very lively manner.

A rebel deserter who came in a day or two ago reports that he was one of the squad that was unfortunately fired upon by one of our howitzers a few days ago, under the supposition that they were rebels. He also reports that the man whom one of our videttes saw suspended to an apple-tree was one of his companions who had been captured by a rebel cavalryman and summarily executed.

APRIL 9.

The rebel batteries kept pretty busy yesterday, but attracted little notice from the gunboats. Four new rebel batteries were discovered on this side the river, about twelve hundred yards east of our most eastern blockhouse. They are intended to command our fort. Two of them are thought to contain one small gun each, the third, a twelve-pounder, and the fourth a siege gun. The enemy have one thirty-two-pounder on the other side of the river, but we doubtless outnumber them in heavy artillery. They will find Fort Washington a hard nut, and there are heavier pieces on board the gunboats than have yet disturbed the echoes hereabout. All Commodore Renshaw asks is a land force to capture the rebel guns after he has dismounted them. Such a force we hope is not far distant. The music of their artillery is reported to have been heard yesterday and last night.

Yesterday we witnessed the affecting scene of a soldier's funeral at our blockhouse. The deceased was Isaac Powers, of Co. B, Mass. 27th, who met his death by falling down a flight of stairs in the blockhouse. At the close of the services, the deep boom of the rebel siege gun came across the water with thrilling effect. The peculiarity and danger of our situation were earnestly alluded to by Chaplain Woodworth, as an incentive to preparation for the great change which in the fortunes of war so soon might visit a large number of us.

This morning (and this is to be the rule during the present condition of affairs) we were called out for roll-call between three and four o'clock, and then stationed behind the breastworks until sunrise. We are living upon three-quarters rations, but thus far have kept hunger well at bay. Gen. Foster has taken possession of all provisions for sale in Washington, and says we can subsist on them thirty or forty days. We have despatched a few cattle, but the meat is poor stuff—lean and garlicy—barely fit to eat.

APRIL 10.

Our prospects are brightening. Last night two schooners from Newbern, loaded with ammunition and forage, passed the blockade, and arrived here safely. Those in charge of the vessels inform us that a large force of infantry is on the way by land from Newbern.

Contrabands who came in yesterday, report the rebels confident of having us in their power, and as saying that they can keep back any reinforcements which may be sent to us.

The 44th Regiment has met with an irreparable loss in the death of its excellent surgeon, Dr. Ware, who expired this morning, after a painful sickness of several days. His disease is supposed to have been the malarious fever peculiar to this locality, but it is suggested that death was hastened by the heavy artillery firing this morning incident to the opening of new rebel batteries on a hill east of the town. One week ago no event could have been more unexpected by us. With a frame compact, sinewy and nervous, Dr. Ware was the apparent embodiment of physical health. His, surely, we thought, was a constitution firm and elastic enough to withstand not only the effects of the climate but of professional labors made doubly severe by an assiduity and tenderness which had won the affection and the *reverence* of the whole regiment. But death, mindless of all human calculations, has ended the life and usefulness of Dr. Ware at a time which adds peculiar providential mystery to the event, inasmuch as the necessity of his skillful ministrations was perhaps never more imminent than at the moment of his death. This, however, is not the chief reason why we lament his death. We mourn the loss of the true, inestimable man, more than that of the able, experienced surgeon. Dr. Ware was the son of the venerable Dr. Robert Ware, of Boston.

APRIL 11.

For the last two mornings the rebel batteries to the east have performed lively reveilles. Fort Washington, in the centre of our outward line of entrenchments, was the object of their attention ; but several shells have reached our extreme left, a piece of one striking close to the shanties of Company D's boys, bounding thence into the river. The fort replies to these sallies with excellent effect, and always has the last word, the rebels withdrawing. Thus far the number of our wounded is extremely small, and the gratifying fact is doubtless in a measure due to the traverses which intersect the outer breastwork, thereby preventing the unpleasant effects of a raking fire parallel with the entrenchments. Yesterday some of Company A's shelter tents were riddled while the boys were safe behind their traverse. Besides this defence, we are still more securely guarded against the rebel artillery from the east by bomb-proofs on the western side of the traverses. We found it practicable to avail ourselves of their protection this morning, but we enlivened the chilly gloom of the retreat by singing various choice *arias* from *Il Recruitio.*

Between the building and turfing of earthworks, bomb-proofs, standing guard and doing nightly picket duty, we are kept pretty hard at work, and are beginning to feel the combined effects of hard knocks and poor rations. We have considerable use for lumber, and Grist's cotton mill and other out-buildings are levied upon accordingly. Having secured the boards and joists, we transport them to the fortifications upon the wheels of Grist's old family carriage. Since this man left town, renewed suspicions of thorough treachery have taken possession of the soldiers, and the Grist mansion itself would hardly be safe if the red hospital flag did not wave over it.

This morning the music of a rebel band floated to our ears from over the river. This afternoon we have had the thorough bass of their big guns on the same side, sending bomb-shells into town. And no reinforcements yet! We are very anxious to see them, but not greatly surprised at their non-arrival, considering the lions they will find in their way, in the shape of unbridged streams, fallen trees, and rebel forts and rifle-pits.

Attached to some of the oblong shells which were sent into town this morning, were some of the Shenckl percussion fuses, bearing the mark of George H. Fox & Co., of Boston, manufacturers. Perhaps the gentlemen of this firm will be interested in the fact. Boston boys think it a little funny to meet such specimens of home manufacture in North Carolina.

A night or two ago our pickets on the Jamesville road got beyond the outposts of the enemy, and had an unexpected rencounter with the rebel pickets. The interview was quite cordial, but our boys were assured that the rebs had Washington in a vice. Many inside are of the same opinion, but of course this depends upon the success we may have in getting reinforcements through.

Night before last it was reported that the rebels were crossing the river above and below us, on flat-boats, with a view of strengthening themselves on the south side, to meet our reinforcements from Newbern. We also have rumors of fights on the Newbern road.

APRIL 14.

Last night steamers from below with reinforcements of men and provisions ran by the rebel batteries under a hot fire, and arrived safely at Washington. Our garrison is now strong, and our friends need have no fears concerning us. We are in the receipt of letters and papers to the 3d inst.

It is said that the long delay in sending us reinforcements was caused by their repulse by the rebels on the Newbern road. But of this matter I can only give you rumors. You can imagine that the loyal part of Little Washington is jubilant to-day.

------

WASHINGTON, N. C., APRIL 16, 1863.

My diary of the siege of Washington, forwarded to you by a steamer which left on the 14th, closed on the 13th, when I announced the gratifying intelligence of the arrival of reinforcements. Yesterday morning General Foster departed for Newbern, leaving behind the following general order :

HEADQUARTERS 18TH ARMY CORPS, ⎱
WASHINGTON, N. C., APRIL 14TH, 1863. ⎰

The Commanding General announces to the garrison of this town that he is about to leave for a brief space of time the gallant soldiers and sailors of this garrison. Brigadier General Potter will remain in command, and in him the Commanding General has the most perfect confidence as a brave and able soldier. The command of the naval forces remains unchanged ; therefore that arm of the service will be as effective and perfect as heretofore. The Commanding General leaves temporarily, and for the purpose of putting himself at the head of a relieving force. Having raised the siege, he expects soon to return ; but before leaving he must express to the naval force here, and to the soldiers under his command, the 27th and 44th Massachusetts Regiments, detachments of the 3d New York Cavalry and 1st North Carolina Volunteers, his thanks for and admiration of the untiring zeal, noble emulation and excellent courage which have distinguished them during the sixteen days of the enemy's attack on this post ; and he feels confident that the display of those qualities under General Potter will hold the place till the siege be raised.

J. G. FOSTER,
Gen. Commanding 18th Army Corps.

Regimental glorification is so prevalent a weakness on the part of newspaper correspondents in the army, that I am almost ashamed to state a fact which I know will be pleasing to our friends at home. I allude to a marked unofficial compliment from General Foster, who observed to Colonel Lee that the 44th regiment has performed more service than any other nine months' regiment in his department, and probably more than any other nine months' regiment in the field ; that the conduct of the regiment had been in every respect spirited, honorable and gratifying to him.    I offer this as a most thorough refutation of the villainous libels which the low enmity of a few men in the other Massachusetts regiments have dictated and set afloat.

The air is full of rumors discreditable to the generalship and bravery of General Spinola, who was last week sent from Newbern to relieve this garrison, in which attempt, it is reported, he miserably failed, and then fell back without a sufficient cause.    If he has not done his duty, General Foster will be the last man to excuse the omission.    He has chafed like a caged lion during the siege, and is said to have gone away mad as a March hare.    The rebels did not omit the customary salute when his steamer passed down the river, and it is thought one or more cannon balls went through the upper works of the vessel.    At the same time the rebel batteries to the east of the town played upon us in a lively manner, and sent us into our bomb-proofs upon the double-quick. The rebels amused themselves in the same manner on the previous morning, about the time the band was giving expression to our joy at receiving reinforcements, and in fact this has been the order of the day for a long time.    But it has been no boys' play.    Shot and shell have rained all along our line.    Several of our shelter tents have been cut to pieces by them.    I could recount scores of " miraculous escapes."    Our bomb-proofs have probably been the means of saving many lives.    It certainly seems scarcely short of Providential interposition that a bombardment extending over sixteen days has not resulted in the loss of a single life or limb on our side.

This morning five deserters have come in and report the rebels falling back on Greenville.    The indications confirm the report.

Cavalry and infantry scouts find their breastworks this side of the river abandoned, and the rebs have not fired a gun to-day on either side. A thunder tempest raged last night, and it is highly probable that they skedaddled under the protection which the noise of the elements afforded them.    Finding the blockade ineffective, they despaired of starving us out, and so have retired with great loss—of ammunition.    In this respect it has been a very expensive siege to them : and it is believed that their loss in lives has not been inconsiderable.    They have found Little Washington, under the engineering of General Foster, a hard nut to crack, and will scarce try the experiment again.

P. M. Our gunboats hammered away at the positions lately held by the rebels on the south side of the river, until being satisfied that they were no longer there, boats were sent to reconnoitre about Rodman's Point. It happened that a few of the enemy, probably their rear guard, were still on the ground. They rose and fired on our boats with fatal effect. An engineer of the gunboat Ceres was killed. Frank Tripp, of Company E, 43d regiment, in another boat, was very severely wounded. The boats then withdrew.

This morning our scouts visited the scene of the principal rebel bivouac this side the river, and came to the conclusion that about two thousand men had encamped there.

Towards night the gunboats Hunchback, Southfield and two or three others, which during the siege had been hanging ten miles below, came up in range of Rodman's Point, and commenced shelling the woods with great vigor. The same amount of firing in the same places yesterday or day before would have placed the rebels in great danger of their limbs and lives; but before opening his fire the magnanimous commander of the down river fleet waited until our erring brethren had got beyond the reach of the Hunchback's hundred pounders, and then blazed away, to the mingled admiration and terror of the contraband population of Washington and vicinity. I am informed that the timely arrival of the Rhode Island 5th, which gallantly ran the blockade on the night of the 13th, was solely due to the energetic determination of Colonel Sisson, in opposition to the naval authorities down the river. In other respects a night-mare retardation has seemed to characterize all attempts to relieve this garrison.

---

HILL'S POINT, 8 MILES BELOW WASHINGTON, N. C.,  
SOUTH SIDE OF SOUND, APRIL 17, 1863.

Companies C, D, and I were ordered on board the gunboat Eagle last evening, where we slept. This morning we landed in small boats at this place. It was the strongest point of the rebel blockade. Behind the earthworks, which were mostly erected at an early day in the rebellion, are a plenty of bomb-proofs. The natural defences of the place are remarkable for this flat vicinity. Behind the earthworks is a pleasant piece of table-land, which we now occupy. Between the shore and the woods is a rebel rifle-pit. This forenoon we skirmished out a a mile or so, encountering an old rebel camp and the one the rebels have recently occupied. We picked up one butternut gentleman with

a carpet bag containing a rebel uniform, and the picture of a rebel officer.  Butternut said he picked up the carpet bag in the woods as he was
going home from mill.  He said the rebs were robbing the population
of their provisions and had nearly cleaned him out.  There was a
" right smart" of rebs here, but they left in a hurry night before last.
Three companies of the 43d, C, D and H, landed here from schooners
about noon.  They had been lying below the blockade for a week or
so, with the other companies of their regiment, who had been suddenly
called back to Newbern.  The 43d formed part of Spinola's late expedition, and the boys of that regiment are emphatic in their denunciation
of the conduct of the General in retreating without, as they say, sufficient cause.  Their march back, after getting within ten miles of Newbern, was of the most forced and exhausting description.  The affair
will probably be investigated by a court martial.

The excellent sketch of our situation and defences at Washington,
which accompanies this letter, was drawn by George W. Hight, of
Company D.  I have no doubt you will take pleasure in showing it to
any friend of the 44th regiment who may call for that purpose.

APRIL 18, 1863.

The detachment of the 44th Regiment stationed at this point are
quite delighted with their situation.  We have seen nothing so pleasant
in North Carolina.  The Tar river here widens into Pamlico Sound,
and from our position on this bluff or table land, it spreads out before
us like a beautiful lake in the woods.  This morning, one of the love-
liest of Spring, the air is fragrant with pines and flowers, and melo-
dious with the songs of birds.  The field is dotted with fruit trees in
bloom.  Yesterday we found the woods spangled with jasmine, violets,
box and dog-wood, and our skirmishers with their hands full of flowers
looked more like a Maying party than soldiers expecting a foe in every
bush.  A rebel soldier lies buried beneath a branching cedar close to
our bivouac, the living and the dead sleeping together.  Upon the
headboard of the latter we read " Henry Davenport, 52d North Carolina Regiment."  His resting place was selected with true refinement
of taste.

APRIL 20.

From our picket post yesterday we caught the sound of wild cheering, which we soon learned was given to the advance of our army from
Newbern, headed by General Foster.  To-day we learn that three of
our brigades are in Washington, another in the vicinity of Kinston,
and another between here and Newbern.  Feint movements are per-

haps involved in this disposition of troops, but we have no idea of what
General Foster is about.  He is reinforced by the return of part of his
troops from the Department of the South, including the Massachusetts
23d and the New Jersey 9th.  The Massachusetts 24th and the Connecticut 10th are still with General Hunter.

We are in receipt to-day of letters from the North, containing newspaper slips devoted to late affairs in this vicinity.  The letter of a correspondent at Newbern, which the Boston Journal accepts as " the
clearest account of affairs at Washington and Newbern," is a complete
tissue of errors, of a character so serious that the regiment has been
excited to indignation by their unfortunate publicity.

The statement that Companies A and D went outside the earthworks
and had their retreat cut off, contains two errors.  Company D did not
go out at all until after the blockade was raised, and the retreat of Company A was not cut off.  The "cutting their way through with the loss
of sixteen" is also a pure fiction, as is the announcement of the death
of Orderly Sergeant Edmands.  Our total loss in the affair alluded to
was three wounded, who were taken prisoners.  Orderly Sergeant Edmands was not one of these, but the careless statement of his death has
doubtless plunged a circle of friends into mourning as sorrowful and
deep, for a time, as the event itself could produce.  Then who shall
undertake to estimate the anxiety and torture of suspense in the minds
of the friends of Companies A and D before they shall find out the
falsity of the story of " sixteen killed?"  Our laws are defective in
their want of penalties for such outrageous sins against the tenderest
and sacredest feelings of nature as those perpetrated by a class of irre-
sponsible correspondents, who seize upon and circulate rumors for facts,
and who mutilate the king's English and human feelings with about
equal facility and *sang froid.*

IN TOW OF STEAMER THOMAS COLLYER, }<br>
WEDNESDAY, APRIL 23, 1863. }

Having contributed to the salvation of Little Washington, we are
now on our way back to the "home camp" at Newbern, leaving Hill's
Point garrisoned by a portion of the 43d, and Washington by several
New York and Pennsylvania regiments, together with the Massachusetts 27th and part of the 43d.  Accompanying us on our way back to
Newbern are five companies of the Rhode Island 5th, and two companies of the Massachusetts 46th.  We have been absent from Newbern
over five weeks, and now the near prospect of getting into our barracks

again has elated every heart. Lots of boxes for us have accumulated in our absence, and our anxiety to be at them is quite intense. We have, to tell the truth, a harrowing suspicion that the invalid guard, actuated by an unselfish purpose to keep them from spoiling, will save us the trouble not only of opening the boxes but of eating the contents. Heaven forbid, however! In our present half-famished condition this is no trifling thought.

---

NEWBERN, APRIL 24.

Here we are at old Newbern again, but not at "home," as we fondly call our old barracks while absent on expeditions. We found the New Jersey 9th in our old quarters, so we betook ourselves to the barracks of our old and beloved neighbors, the Conn. 10th. But we are to stay here only a short time. Saturday we are going down into the city to do provost-guard duty, and shall probably continue in that capacity the remainder of our term of service. We shall there be quartered in houses, and, except in extreme cases, be excused from participating in expeditions. This will please those of our timorous friends who, when we left home, gravely and affectionately admonished us not to get shot. There is now, dear friends, a right smart chance for us to escape rebel bullets, "except," as Sparrowgrass once remarked, "in case of invasion."

APRIL 25.

To-day we were formally installed as provost-guard of Newbern, thereby relieving the 45th regiment, which has for a considerable time been acting in the same capacity. The 45th received us with all the honors, and we stood at present arms as they marched past us in going out of the city. Each regiment bore its regimental colors and was headed by its band.

Our company (D) are put in possession of a commodious wooden mansion and its out-buildings on Pollock street, lately occupied by Co. A, of the 45th. We found the rooms in neat condition, and decorated with wreaths and bouquets of flowers, accompanied by the pleasant salutatory words, "WELCOME 44," several times inscribed on the walls. The "Jolly Five" have the thanks of "Corporal," and his mess for their part in a greeting so graceful on one side and so grateful to the other.

The 54th regiment has made another draft upon the 44th for officers, Charles E. Tucker, Co. E, Willard Howard and Henry W. Littlefield, of Co. D, having just received their commissions as lieutenants in the former. They will leave for Boston to-morrow.

I learn that the officers of our regiment have decided to present to the Fifth Regiment of Rhode Island a stand of colors as a slight acknowledgment of the gallantry of that regiment in running the rebel blockade and coming to our relief at Washington. The Mass. 27th, with whom we were blockaded, is now in Newbern.

APRIL 26.

To-day the regiment have attended the obsequies of our late lamented and beloved Surgeon, Dr. Ware, to whose unexpected death we are none of us quite reconciled. His remains will be carried to Boston by the steamer Ellen S. Terry, which leaves Newbern to-day.

This letter is carried to Boston by H. P. Tuttle, late of the Cambridge Observatory, who has just been discharged from the 44th regiment on account of having received a commission as Assistant Paymaster in the Navy.

————

NEWBERN, N. C., MAY 12, 1863.

Our life as provost guard at Newbern is too uneventful to call for much letter writing. We have been joined by companies B and F, who have been a long while on picket, and we are now a regiment of policemen. The rank and file are on guard almost every other day, and the duty is found at once severe, irksome, and often abhorrent. I am rather glad that our present reputation as policemen is not to be the measure of our characters as soldiers. I am loath to confess that we were getting to be beloved by the tough ones of the old regiments, who, since pay-day, which occurred recently, found three dollars a bottle for whisky no bar to indulgence in that popular stimulant, and who have an acquired loathing of the guard-house. However, we are *becoming* very exemplary policemen, if I may judge from the curses (both loud and deep) which are showered upon the devoted heads of the 44th regiment, and nine months' men generally.

Newbern is looking very attractive. The gardens are still rich with roses of every hue. I wish the paper May-flower girls of Boston could be turned amongst them for a day.

We have small time or opportunity for amusement, although I have no doubt that the shoulder straps find provost-guard life extremely bully, setting aside some of the severe duties which belong to them as moral conservators. They are treated to concerts, attend private

music parties, and regale themselves with ice water,—very good in this
latitude at this season.   The privates are solicited to produce another
opera; and an entertainment of that character, founded upon the siege
of Washington, together with a regimental concert, a dramatic performance, and a *bal masque*, is upon the tapis.

Weddings, white and colored, are just now the subject of gossip.
One of our own corporals has been and gone and done it, and one of
the pretty natives of Newbern is now Mrs. Lawrence.   Last night
some of our boys assisted at a darkey wedding, putting the happy pair
to bed in true traditional style.

Our nights are rendered musical by the plaintive choral hymnings
of devotional negroes in every direction, alone and in groups.   From
their open cabins come the mingled voices of men wrestling painfully
and agonizingly with the spirit, and those uttering the ecstatic notes
of the redeemed.

<hr />

NEWBERN, N. C., MAY 16, 1863.

We are in a state of stagnation.   We have not been so unhappy
since the date of our enlistment as we have since we entered upon the
police business at Newbern.   We have almost forgotten the toil and
misery of long marches and sieges, and revert with something like
regret to the days of active campaigning.   I have no doubt that many
of us will voluntarily return to the army should the state of the country
call for more service at our hands.   We rejoice that we have had a
hand in this glorious contest for the integrity of our country.   No
sacrifice or hardship we have endured balances the gratification of
having done our country some service, however small or humble that
service may have been.   If we had but one word of advice to give the
young men of our acquaintance, it would be to *enlist voluntarily*
while a chance remains to identify yourselves in a glorious warfare
which is evidently drawing to such a termination as every patriot must
pray and fight for.   Do not stand back because you think the danger
is past.   We may safely calculate that much work remains to be done.
The serpent of secession is only scotched, not killed.   The clouds
may yet again lower over us, and every strong arm may be needed to
sweep them away.

How well the magnificent strategy and the more magnificent fighting
of our New England General comports with his clear, ringing testimony
before the Committee on the Conduct of the War!

How stands McClellan presidential stock at the North? Who will heal up the wounds of the copperheads? Nothing will keep them from despair but the injudicious arrest and imprisonment of blatant politicians who hunger and thirst after martyrdom, and who do not know that their advocacy of a cause is its most effective condemnation.

MAY 18.

A "trance medium" by the name of James Richardson, of Athol, in Co. B, 27th regiment, assures the members of his regiment that they will be discharged from the service in less than a year from this time, and that the war will be brought to a close before that time. His associates, although professing to have no faith in asserted revelations of this kind, are forced to confess that Richardson has proved to be a true prophet in several important instances. He foretold the battles of Roanoke and Newbern, and with so many of their particulars as to prove his possession of a power altogether unexplainable. He foretold the siege of Washington by stating that the 27th regiment would take part in a long but not very bloody battle, and that a certain man would be killed. Following this came the seventeen days' siege, and the death of the man alluded to. After this battle he said the regiment would soon remove to another place in transports. That has also happened. From that place, in two or four months, they were to embark in transports for the North.

Orderly Sergeant Stebbins of Co. F has been commissioned as second lieutenant in place of Lieut. Hartwell, now a captain in the 54th. Lieut. Stebbins is a much esteemed officer, capable and prompt, without being a tyrant or a martinet.

Private Melville, of Co. A, died on Friday of inflammation of the bowels. Since our return from Washington, most of the regiment have been much troubled with diarrhœa, which, however, is now subsiding. The average health of the regiment is good. Dr. Fisher, assistant surgeon with the late Dr. Ware, is now surgeon of the regiment. He is a man of much professional skill and faithfulness. His assistant, Dr. McPhee, is winning golden opinions for the same qualities, united with great complaisance to everybody but "niggers." He was with the English army during the Sepoy rebellion.

At dress parade this evening an order, suitably acknowledging the generous gift of $500 at the hands of Mr. Gilmore, for the benefit of the 44th regiment, was read.

NEWBERN, N. C., MAY 23, 1863.

The Newbern markets are points of some interest. What native products are offered for sale here are chiefly brought in small sail vessels from up and down the river, their place of rendezvous being at the foot of Pollock street. Due notice of the arrival of produce being given at the office of the Provost-Marshal, the sale commences, under such restriction as this functionary may have been pleased to prescribe. If the cargo is of eggs, the hospitals and certain functionaries must first be provided for. After this, private soldiers and negroes may be allowed to buy one or two dozens each. The scenes about these market boats are sometimes quite animated and interesting. This morning a boat lay at the wharf with eggs, sweet potatoes and green peas. The butternut skipper and his son were beset in a very confusing manner. First went the green peas, half grown, at fifty cents a peck. Then the eggs at twenty-five cents a dozen. Anxious but patient darkeys of both sexes, ancient and lean Carolinians of the white "persuasion" and doubtful loyalty, eyed the sweet potatoes and bided their doubtful chances.

The only cheap thing in Newbern is fish—drum, sheepshead, trout, herring, &c., caught down the sound. Trout enough for a family dinner can be bought for twenty-five cents. It is very good, and the staple article of food at the restaurants.

A few farmers who were so fortunate as not to live on the line of our expeditionary raids, send in a little honey. Strawberries, also, are occasionally received.

Recruiting for the African brigade is progressing lively and enthusiastically. Quite a recruiting fever has seized the freedmen of Newbern. Recruiting offices will soon be opened at Washington and Plymouth. Four thousand colored soldiers are counted upon in this department. There is likely to be one item of compensation to the Government for holding these posts upon the enemy's soil. It is, indeed, due to the freedmen that we provide these harbors of refuge for those who escape from the rebel lines. There is, perhaps, not a slave in North Carolina who does not know that he may find freedom in Newbern, and thus Newbern may be the Mecca of a thousand noble aspirations. Leave Newbern to the rebels and hope would die out altogether in many a poor trembling heart. Thank God that the noble inspiration of human liberty is with us in this war. It helps us to abide temporary disaster, and is our pledge of final success. But we shall find a path stony and blood-moistened so long as we fail to have mercy

and deal justly with the unoffending people who are the innocent cause
of this war.

The regimental band of the 44th has grown into a fine institution
under the combined labors of our chief musician, Mr. Babcock, and
the leader, Mr. N. H. Ingraham. Their repertory of music is large
and fine and played with expression. Much of it was arranged by A.
W. Ingraham, a brother of the leader, who has recently visited us. A
third brother, also a member of the band, died in hospital last winter.
Very much is due to this musical trio, and perhaps not less to the fine
orchestral taste of Mr. Babcock, for the striking proficiency attained
by the band. Considering the excellent moral effect of good music in
camp, we can hardly overestimate the thoughtful generosity of those
friends who provided us with musical instruments. If "sounds of
home" by them invoked have kept a single heart from going astray,
the gift could not have been amiss.

Two hundred rebel prisoners, including a Colonel and several line
officers, have just been captured near Kinston, by a brigade under
command of Col. Jones, of the Pennsylvania 58th. Beside the 58th,
the Mass. 5th and 27th took part in the expedition. We had a few
men wounded. The rebels suffered much more.

------

NEWBERN, N. C., MAY 20, 1863.

Your correspondent with the Eighteenth Army Corps proposes to
deliver a series of "lectures upon the war" after he shall have returned to Boston. The topics to be embraced in the proposed series
will include not only operations in the Department of North Carolina,
but in those of the South and Gulf, if not in Virginia and the South-
west, his observations having convinced him that it is by no means
necessary to see a battle to describe it with all desirable particularity
and enthusimoosy. Tickets will be placed at one dollar. Your correspondent undertakes this disinterested and benevolent enterprise in
consequence of the great dearth of information with reference to the
war; but preliminary to his appearance he wishes to engage the services of the experienced dramatic editor of the Boston Herald for a
proper introduction in his new capacity to the Athenian world. He
will understand the importance of a suitable *invitation*, and will please
allow your correspondent to refer him to a formula among the advertisements in Boston papers of a late date. To the document, modelled
according to this suggestion, he will then secure the autographs of

Honorable Edward Everett, Honorable Robert C. Winthrop, *et id omnes genus*, by means of which those eminently respectable gentlemen will be made to express the deep interest with which they have perused the letters of "Corporal" in the Boston Herald, and their burning anxiety to hear him continue his elucidation of such noble themes as bal masques, hard tack, camp opera, salt horse, &c., &c. The dramatic editor, after reference to another formula among the advertisements of late Boston papers, will then indite a noble reply to the invitation, expressing the willingness of "Corporal" to give a public recital of his experience with hard tack, musty rice and shrivelled beans, during the period that he stood up for his country. He may mention June 17th as the time, and Faneuil Hall as the place. This "Interesting Correspondence" must then be published in all the Boston papers, free, if possible, but if not possible, regardless of expense. It is not expected that Faneuil Hall will contain the crowd which will be attracted to its portals; but the public, being a capricious, theatre-going monster, may not turn out as anticipated, so, Mr. Dramatic Editor, I charge you to secure, by a bribe, the attendance of a reporter from each Boston paper, so that the aforesaid monster shall not go unlightened by the oral disquisitions of your correspondent.

The fly-statistics of your Port Royal correspondent must not lead your readers to suppose that the Department of the South enjoys a monopoly of this interesting insect. I allude to common house flies. Fleas and musquitoes do not greatly abound at Newbern, but house flies swarm like the locusts of Egypt. The wood-ticks of Hill's Point, which adhered to the cuticle with a death-grasp, deserved a paragraph, but the house flies of Newbern are even a greater nuisance. The printer will not fail to notice the peculiar manner in which they have punctuated this sheet of manuscript. Their tracks are visible upon every object which they can touch—upon our plates, dippers, knives, forks, bread. They attack us with desperation at meal times, and if we have anything better than usual they are sure to find it out, and rally upon the sweet point, so that while we convey the food to our mouth with one hand, we are forced to fight flies with the other. "Tempus fugit," commences a letter of your Newbern correspondent, "Tiger." "Fly time—very appropriate," parenthetically remarked the free translator Frederick, as he read and described curves in the air.

Among recent visitors here have been Hon. Mr. Comins and wife, of Roxbury. General Wild and staff, of the African brigade, in process of formation, are here.

The recent dash by one of our brigades near Kinston, which resulted in the capture of about two hundred rebel soldiers, was followed by an angry spite on the part of the rebels in that direction, who gave our pickets some trouble, and who, by the agency of a sharpshooter, succeeded in killing Colonel Jones, of the Penn. 58th — one of the most brave officers and excellent men in the service; one of the Jackson type of soldiers, fighting heart and hand, and praying also for the success of the Union cause. We hate to lose such men. We have none such to spare. We wonder that a good cause is bereft of such auxiliaries, and are perhaps too slow to learn the lesson that individual men are of little account in eliminating the grand designs of Providence. We need to be cured of hero-worship. It has been one of the banes interfering with the due progress of the war. We may safely put faith in men collectively, and in the principles which prevade the masses of the North, but never in any single man or set of men.

Company F, Captain Storrow has gone to Fortress Monroe, having in charge a lot of rebel prisoners. We expect the company will come back to Newbern and accompany the regiment home.

Another levy has been made upon us for officers in regiments of colored men. Privates W. D. Crane of Company D, Goodwin, Woodward, and Sergeant Weld, of Company F, are among those who propose leaving Newbern for Boston to-day to take commisions as line officers in one or more of these regiments.

Some of the more festive of the line officers in this department have recently assisted at a variegated affair called a nigger ball, which transpired at the house of Black Lovinia, one of the Skittletop sisterhood. Not the least interested and observant spectators of this *recherche* affair were one or two sentinels in the vicinity, who tell curious stories of the carryings-on. The assemblage occupied two stories of the building, the lower rooms being partly devoted to dancing; but some of the movements were not recognized in any of the modern schottisches, waltzes, or polka-redowas. It was a marbled crowd, the upper stratum being described as yellow and white, and the lower one pure black and white. So, with strange indifference to the articles of war, say those prying fellows, the nocturnal sentinels.

The rebel guerrillas, who are always prowling around Newbern, succeeded recently in catching a couple of schooners becalmed down the river, and burned them to the water's edge.

Our convalescents are sent down to Beaufort and Morehead City for the benefit to be derived from sea air. The principal hospital was formerly a large hotel. It stands upon piles, and the tides flow beneath it. The patients ride in sail boats, eat strawberries, and disport with the fair secesh of Beaufort, who are quite an improvement upon the tallow-faced damsels of the interior.

------

NEWBERN, N. C., MAY 29, 1863.

As our nine months' service draws to its close, time drags its slow length along in the most irritating manner possible. This police life would soon demoralize, if it did not kill us quite. We have already lost not a little of our former excellency in drill, and we have dubious anticipations as to the figure we shall cut on Boston Common.

If we arrive in Boston before the expiration of our term of service, there is a probability of our spending a few days in camp at Readville, where we hope to recover our military stamina, and where we shall be at home to our old friends of blessed memory.

In a recent letter containing a reference to the band, I said that we had been visited by A. W. Ingraham, to whose skillful arrangement of music, much of the excellency of the band was due. Mr. Ingraham has since the assumed the leadership, and his splendid bugle playing is now a marked and attractive feature of the music at serenades and dress parades.

On the 27th our regiment being formally mustered agreeable to an order from headquarters, we were addressed by General Foster and solicited to join the new heavy artillery regiment. The General was heartily cheered, but I think very few of the boys will care to re-enlist until they have seen Massachusetts once more, although furloughs and other inducements are tendered. The artillery branch of the service. the Department of North Carolina, and General Foster are all to the liking of our regiment, and many of its members are likely to return here.

The 27th was General Foster's birthday. In the evening his residence was brilliantly lighted and crowded with guests. Music, gaiety and splendid hospitality graced the occasion—contrasting strangely with the impressive ceremonials of the preceding day attending the removal of the remains of Colonel Jones to the steamer.

Captain Smith, of Company H, Lieutenants Newell, of Company E, and Odiorne, of Company G, Orderly Sergeant White, of Company E, Orderly Sergeant Cunningham, of Company C, and private Curtis, of Company F, are to take commissions in a new regiment of heavy artillery recruiting for this garrison, and to be under the command of Major Frankle, of the Massachusetts 17th regiment, as Colonel.

Orderly Sergeant Mulliken, of Company H, has been elected Second Lieutenant, in place of Lieutenant Howe, promoted to be First Lieutenant, in place of Lieutenant Johnson, appointed Adjutant, in place of Lieutenant Hinkley, who is to be Adjutant of the artillery regiment. Since writing the above, I learn that a number of our regiment, as well as a number in the 43d and 45th, have decided to join as privates.

---

NEWBERN, N. C., JUNE 1, 1863.

By a blunder of the printer, I was made in a recent letter to allude to Lieut. Col. Hartwell, of the Mass. 55th, as a former *second* lieutenant of Co. F. He was first lieutenant of that company, and much distinguished as a disciplinarian, as well as for his moral qualities.

Intelligence has just been received here of the death in a rebel hospital of Orderly Sergeant Hobart, of Co. G, who was wounded and captured near Washington, March 30, at the commencement of the siege of that place. This intelligence comes by way of Washington, D. C., through official sources. Nothing is known here of the fate of private Leonard, who was severely wounded and captured at the same time.

Some objection is made to the use of the word "police," as descriptive of our duties in Newbern. I have used it in the civil and not in the military sense of the word. Police duty, in a military sense, is the duty of cleaning up the camp. As provost-guard of Newbern, our duty is to "clean out" disreputable places, to see that soldiers in town are not absent from their regiments without leave, and to attend to moral publicans generally.

The negroes here honor the Hibernian custom of "waking" their dead. On occasions of this sort, they sometimes render night so hideous by their songs and shoutings that the guard is attracted to the scene of their spiritual orgies, to enforce order. At midnight, the revellers solemnly refresh themselves with coffee, and then resume their howling, reciting and chanting simple hymns, line by line.

Several transports are lying here and at Morehead, in one of which a cavalry company arrived on the 29th ult. On the same day, Co. F returned from Fortress Monroe, whither they had been sent to guard prisoners sent from Newbern. Another transport arrived yesterday with more cavalry.

Lieuts. Briggs and Field, detached from the regiment some months ago to serve on the signal corps in the Department of the South, have returned to Newbern, and will go home with the regiment. Detailed men are ordered to report to their companies on or before the 8th, about the time we are expected to leave for home. It is said all our sick will be taken with us. Even the most protracted cases of "convalescence" at Beaufort will hardly forego the glory of "marching up State street," the only avenue to Boston by which a returning regiment could possibly get into the city. Will the great army of quidnuncs, the men with green spectacles, umbrellas and towering shirt collars, coatless quill-drivers, the breechless admirers of brass bands, and the floating population generally take the hint? What avails going to the war if there can be no State street *finale* with the customary remarks of the reporters so nicely adjusted to the merits of each individual corps? How inscrutable are the judgments of reporters until their impressions come to light in good fair type, when we find that the last regiment, like all the preceding ones, "looked finely and marched like veterans!" Of course we shall be proud to be noticed; and if the great army of sight-seers, (without whom "marching up State street" would be as apples of Sodom,) shall really enjoy the coming novelty of a regiment marching up State street, will voluntarily swell the number of those soon to march *down* street, we shall feel more than paid for having afforded them a sensation, at the expense of our blushing modesty.

JUNE 6, 1863.

At this writing (half past one o'clock P. M.) the 44th regiment, pleasantly quartered on board the transport steamers "Guide" and "George Peabody," is steaming out of Beaufort (N.C.) harbor, bound for dear old Boston. Just as the train of open cars which bore us from Newbern to Morehead City this morning was getting under way, the clouds opened with rain as though determined to treat us with a parting baptism, as well as the introductory one by which we were drenched through and through on our way from Morehead City to Newbern last October. But in this respect we were agreeably disappointed. It rained but little, and the sunbeams came through so many vapory clouds that the weather was delightful. Nine months' absence from the sea coast had sharpened an old love for ocean breezes; and as we neared Morehead, the sweet smells of the beach mingled with the refreshing coolness coming

"From where old Triton blows his wreathed horn,"

were inhaled with delight and gratitde.

The right wing of our regiment is on board the Guide. The right wing includes companies A, G, H, K, and E. The Colonel, Lieut.-Colonel, and Major, the regimental band, the surgeon, and the sick, are also on board the Guide.

The left wing is upon the George Peabody. We consist of companies F, B, D, C, and I, under command of senior Captain Storrow.

Being the slower boat, we have the start. The weather continues delightful; the sea is azure: and, as we turn our prow northward, satisfaction and joyful anticipations hover over us beautiful as birds of paradise.

I believe we carry with us from the department of North Carolina the cordial good will of Gen. Foster. That this sentiment is fully reciprocated by our regiment the enthusiasm in its ranks always excited by the presence of the General is abundant proof. He honored the occasion of our departure by coming out to the depot with his full staff. He was greeted with a storm of cheers, which he and staff heartily returned. Last night he received our officers at his residence in a very complimentary manner. In the meantime the quarters of several of the companies were illuminated, the boys exchanged visits in a very unceremonious and jubilant manner, and cheered everybody and everything without regard to sex or condition. So passed the eve of our departure from Newbern. This morning the Mass. 3d regiment, Captain Richmond, honored us by escorting the 44th to the depot.

We are succeeded as provost guard by the Mass. 27th, one of the noblest bodies of men in the service.

JUNE 7, 1863.

We had heavy showers and a high wind last night. Many of the deck sleepers were driven below. Those who remained found their clothes and blankets saturated with water this morning. Our guns, late the pride of the regiment, were covered with rust. A stiff wind was blowing from the northwest, and the unsteady motion of the boat was beginning to have the customary effect on landsmen. We turned out this morning a dismal-looking set; but, as the day advanced, we presently discovered blue sky enough to make a pair of breeches for a Dutchman, and then we knew we were safe, according to the best marine logic. Still later the sun struggled into view, cheering our hearts and drying our blankets at the same time. Contrary to the general impression, I find that there was but little sea-sickness last night. It was something else,—sourness of the stomach, sickness of the stomach, headache, &c., but the symptoms were wonderfully uniform.

On board the George Peabody, with our left wing, are about one hundred men from the 46th, 43d, 8th, and other Massachusetts nine months' regiments, going home on a furlough, having enlisted in Col. Frankle's regiment of heavy artillery, at Newbern.

JUNE 9.

The interim indicated by my last two dates was covered by indisposition—not sea-sickness, of course, but something mightily like it in all its external indications. I may here mention that we have had a pretty rough trip, steaming for most of the time directly against a northeaster. As a natural result, thirteen were in the hospital last night, and the venerable captain of the Peabody was forced to retire to his cabin and solemnly take an observation through the skylight every thirty minutes.

We have been cheered by one reminiscence of camp life, to wit, roll-call. The homeward-bound citizen soldiery, thinking routine about played out, answered *en masse* for every name as it was called, and found it impossible, in consequence of the roughness of the sea, to keep from tumbling over each other, to the great detriment of the proper company rectilinear. Roll-call on shipboard was thenceforward dispensed with as impracticable, if not impossible. It was with no small satisfaction that our eyes opened this morning to find the Peabody making its way up Vineyard Sound, between beautiful, bold, green shores dotted with villages and more scattered white cottages, eloquent of thrift and industry which cannot live with slavery and rebellion.

7 O'CLOCK, P. M.

We were steaming up in the track of a golden sunset this evening toward dear old Boston, when our progress was arrested by a terrible being on a tug-boat, who first demanded the name of our regiment, and then ordered us to haul to. We obeyed. We then inquired of the terrible being, who wore two rows of brass buttons, if our escort, the Guide, had arrived? "Who is the officer in command?" again demanded the being, not choosing to hear the question. He was informed. The being then boarded us, waving us from before him with both hands. He retired to the cabin for a conference, and presently emerged therefrom, but what is to come of all this we can only conjecture with fear and trembling. We may have to wait on board for the Guide, which we now for the first time are apprised, is behind us, but there is a talk of putting us into Fort Independence. Of one thing, however, we are sure : We have seen Major-Generals and even a Major-General of an Army Corps, but General Foster, in all his glory, can hold no candle to the terrible being who come upon us from the tug.

# THE WELCOME HOME.

The Boston Herald, of June 10th, gives the following account of the welcome home extended to the 44th Regiment:

## THE RECEPTION OF THE FORTY-FOURTH REGIMENT.

As was anticipated, the transport steamer Guide, with the right wing of the 44th regiment, arrived here about 6 o'clock this morning, and steamed directly up to Central Wharf, followed by the George Peabody, and without loss of time the troops commenced to disembark, this work being finished in less than two hours, when the two vessels left the wharf.

The regiment was drawn up by companies, and arms were stacked and knapsacks unslung, when the men were dismissed, a guard being mounted across the wharf. But, prior to this, a large number of men had run up in town to see their friends, supposing their leave allowed them this privilege, and those who did not take this view of the matter remained on the wharf, where hundreds of their friends went to welcome them home.

Soon after the men landed, through the forethought and liberality of Messrs. S. J. Whall and L. M. Dyer, the men were supplied with excellent hot coffee and bread and butter, and thanks to these gentlemen were in every soldier's mouth.

A pleasant incident occurred last evening as the steamer George Peabody, with the left wing of the regiment on board, was passing Fort Warren. The entire garrison turned out and gave continuous cheers of welcome to the returning soldiers, the post band playing "Home, sweet Home." The cheers were returned from the steamer, and were continued until the steamer got a long distance past the fort.

The following is the Roster of the regiment. Several changes have taken place during the term of service of the regiment:

### FIELD AND STAFF.

Colonel, Francis L. Lee; Lieutenant Colonel, E. C. Cabot; Major, C. W. Dabney, Jr.; Surgeon, T. W. Fisher; Assistant Surgeon, Daniel McPhee; Adjutant, E. C. Johnson; Quartermaster, F. Bush, Jr.; Chaplain, E. H. Hall.

*Non-Commissioned Staff.*—Sergeant Major, Wm. H. Bird; Quartermaster's Sergeant, F. S. Gifford; Commissary's Sergeant, C. D. Woodberry; Hospital Steward, W. C. Brigham; Principal Musician, G. L. Babcock.

### LINE OFFICERS.

*Captains*—Company A, J. M. Richardson; B, J. M. Griswold; C, G. B. Lombard; D, H. D. Sullivan; E, S. W. Richardson; F, C. Storrow; G, C. Hunt; H, W. V. Smith; I, J. R. Kendall; K, R. H. Weld.

*First Lieutenants*—Company A, J. Coffin; B, J. A. Kendrick; Jr.; C, W. Hedge; D, J. H. Blake, Jr.; E, J. S. Newell; F, T. E. Tay-

lor; G, J. C. White; H, A. R. Howe; I, W. D. Hooper; K, F. T.
Brown.

*Second Lieutenants*—Company A, C. G. Kendall; B, C. C. Soule:
C, J. W. Briggs: D, A. H. Stebbins; E, J. S. Cumston; F, H. S.
Stebbins; G, F. Odiorne; H, J. L. Mulliken; J, B. F. Fields, Jr.;
K, J. Parkinson, Jr.

The regiment has been in five engagements, viz.: Rawls' Mills, Kinston, Whitehall, Goldsboro' and Washington, all in North Carolina, in
which thirteen men were killed.  On leaving Massachusetts there was
an aggregate of 1018 in the regiment, and it returns with 916, one
hundred and two men having been killed in battle, died from disease or
been discharged for disability.

Prior to the departure of the regiment from Newbern, the following
order was issued by Major General Foster, which shows how well the
men have served their country during their term of service:

HEADQUARTERS 18TH ARMY CORPS, 

NEWBERN, N. C., JUNE 5TH, 1863. 

Special Orders No. 160—17.

The Commanding General, on bidding farewell to the 44th Regiment M. V. M.
conveys to them his high appreciation of and thanks for their services whilst in
this Department.

As a part of the garrison of Washington, and in the various duties to which
they have been assigned, they have always done their duty as soldiers.

The Commanding General in parting expresses his hopes to officers and men
that he may have the pleasure of welcoming their return here, and tenders
them, one and all, his best and kindest wishes for the future.

By command of MAJOR GENERAL J. G. FOSTER.

(Signed)            S. HOFFMAN, A. A. G.

The escort assembled on the Tremont street Mall of the Common,
and at 10 o'clock left there for Central Wharf.  The companies forming the escort were under command of Major J. Putnam Bradlee, and
consisted of the New England Guard Reserve with 93 guns; the Massachusetts Rifle Club, Captain Moore, with 114 guns: the Battalion of
National Guards, Major C. W. Stevens, with 102 guns, and the Roxbury Reserve Guard, Captain Wyman, with 80 guns; the whole headed
by Gilmore's and the Brigade Bands.

On reaching Central wharf the escort was drawn up in line along
India street, and the Regiment being formed on the wharf, the usual
preliminary proceedings to the taking up the escort were gone through
with, and the column moved over the prescribed route to the Common,
entering at the gate at the corner of Charles and Beacon streets.

All along the route the streets were crowded to excess, and the windows were filled with ladies, who cheered the men with a will as they
marched along.  Bouquets were showered on them from every side,
and the entire march was an ovation of which the regiment must have
felt proud.

After entering the parade ground the regiment marched past the

escort and then wheeled into line in front, the right resting on Beacon
street mall.  The Mayor and City Government were in waiting in front
of the regiment, and Colonel Lee having opened his ranks and saluted,
brought his men to the "parade rest."  His Honor Mayor Lincoln then
advanced in front of the line, being accompanied by General Tyler,
Chairman of the Committee of Arrangements, and addressed Colonel
Lee as follows :

Mr. Commander:—In behalf of the Municipal Government and the
people of Boston, it is my duty and privilege to extend to you and
your command, the 44th Regiment of Massachusetts Volunteers, a cordial and hearty welcome on your return home from the seat of war.  The
presence of this large assembly, the crowds of citizens who have greeted
you in our thronged streets, the eager impatience with which your
arrival has been anticipated, is an evidence that this is not merely an
official act of common courtesy and form.  The peculiar circumstances
under which your regiment was organized, the character, education and
social position of the young men who compose its rank and file, the
alacrity with which they rallied to arms upon the call of the President,
last summer, the good order which has distinguished them in the camp,
and the valor and gallant deeds which they have shown in the field,
have awakened an unusual interest in the community of which they
form a part.

It has been said that a nation could not rely for defence, in time of
danger, upon the young men brought up in a city.  The habits and as-
sociations of a metropolitan life it was feared unfitted them for those
stern duties and personal physical labors which they must endure in a
soldiers' career, and which their brothers from the agricultural districts,
on account of their accustomed avocations, were better calculated to
perform.  But the experience of the past two years has conquered that
prejudice, if it really ever existed to any considerable extent, for we
have found that some of the most gallant achievements of the war have
been by those regiments which have hailed from the cities of the land,
and from young men whose infancy was cradled in luxury and ease.  It
is not always the largest in stature, or those whose muscles are the best
developed, but it is the *spirit* in the man which commands success, and
the homely virtues of pluck and courage are not confined to particular
classes or business pursuits, but exist wherever the true fire of disinterested patriotism inspires the breast.

You went forth to the distant scene of the conflict at a time when you
must have had a full knowledge of the dangers which you were to encounter, and the sacrifices you must make, offering up even your lives,
if need be, to preserve the liberties of your country.  You loved your
homes, you were bound by the tenderest ties of affectionate relatives
and friends, and because those sentiments were so strong in your
breasts you were ready to do, and to dare, anything and everything in
their behalf.

The flag of our country which has floated over you has been the sym-
bol of all that makes life dear, and you have defended it with a resolu-

tion and manliness which has conferred honor upon yourselves, and added renown to the old Commonwealth under whose auspices you went forth to meet the common enemy.

We owe you a debt of gratitude for what you have done ; we know now that we can rely upon you if the occasion should again call for your services. We mourn for the honored dead and would pay our tribute of respect to the memory of your brave comrades who have fallen in battle or who have been struck by disease in the line of their duty, and we would bless the kind Providence which has protected so many to be again united in family circles, and to enjoy the comforts of homes which have been rendered more precious by the sacrifices you have made. In the future you can look back upon the campaign you have past with just pride, and can feel that in this crisis of our nation's history you have acquitted yourselves like men and patriots.

I cannot conclude without acknowledging the important aid given to your regiment in a perilous period in your history by the 5th Rhode Island Regiment, Col. Sisson, who. I am happy to hear, is present, and can bear to his command the gratitude of our people for their timely assistance.

Having said thus much and congratulated you upon this auspicious occasion, I invite you to the repast which has been prepared and which fair hands are now waiting to serve.

Col. Lee briefly responded, thanking the city authorities for the handsome manner in which the regiment had been received, and expressing the gratification it gave him to be able to bring back so many men. He assured the Mayor that he felt proud of his kind mention of Col. Sisson and the brave 5th Rhode Island Regiment, as his gallant action in the relief of Washington was one of the most noteworthy of the war.

At the close of Col. Lee's response the various companies in the regiment wheeled into platoons and stacked arms, when they were dismissed to partake of the collation, which was spread on separate tables for each company, on the Charles street mall. The tables were tended by ladies, and presented a beautiful appearance from the number of bouquets of flowers adorning them. The Germania Band furnished good music during the time the regiment was partaking of refreshments.

A large crowd assembled on the Common, and after the collation warmly embraced their friends in the regiment.

---

At the conclusion of the ceremonies on the Common, the regiment was granted a furlough until the succeeding Monday at sunset, when they were ordered to report at Readville. On the succeeding Thursday, June 18th, we were mustered out of the service of the United States.